THE BRIDE OF THE INNISFALLEN

and Other Stories

By Eudora Welty

A CURTAIN OF GREEN AND OTHER STORIES
THE ROBBER BRIDEGROOM
THE WIDE NET AND OTHER STORIES
DELTA WEDDING
THE GOLDEN APPLES
THE PONDER HEART
THE BRIDE OF THE INNISFALLEN AND OTHER STORIES
THIRTEEN STORIES
LOSING BATTLES
ONE TIME, ONE PLACE
THE OPTIMIST'S DAUGHTER
THE EYE OF THE STORY
THE COLLECTED STORIES OF EUDORA WELTY
ONE WRITER'S BEGINNINGS

The Bride
of the Innisfallen

AND OTHER STORIES BY

Eudora Welty

A HARVEST/HBJ BOOK

HARCOURT BRACE JOVANOVICH, PUBLISHERS

SAN DIEGO   NEW YORK   LONDON

Requests for permission to make copies of any part of the work should be
mailed to: Permissions, Harcourt Brace Jovanovich, Publishers,
Orlando, FL 32887.

Some of these stories have appeared, a few in different form, in *Accent*,
Harper's Bazaar, and *Sewanee Review*. The following appeared originally in
The New Yorker: "The Bride of the Innisfallen," "No Place for You, My Love,"
and "Kin." For permission to reprint them here the author is grateful to the
editors.

Library of Congress Cataloging in Publication Data
  Welty, Eudora, 1909–
    The bride of the Innisfallen, and other stories.
    "A Harvest/HBJ book."
    I. Title.
  PS3545.E6B7   1985   813'.52   84-22560
  ISBN 0-15-614075-6

PRINTED IN THE UNITED STATES OF AMERICA

F G H I J

TO ELIZABETH BOWEN

CONTENTS

THE BRIDE OF THE INNISFALLEN

and Other Stories

No Place for You, My Love

They were strangers to each other, both fairly well strangers to the place, now seated side by side at luncheon—a party combined in a free-and-easy way when the friends he and she were with recognized each other across Galatoire's. The time was a Sunday in summer—those hours of afternoon that seem Time Out in New Orleans.

The moment he saw her little blunt, fair face, he thought that here was a woman who was having an affair. It was one of those odd meetings when such an impact is felt that it has to be translated at once into some sort of speculation.

With a married man, most likely, he supposed, slipping quickly into a groove—he was long married—and feeling more conventional, then, in his curiosity as she sat there, leaning her cheek on her hand, looking no further before her than the flowers on the table, and wearing that hat.

He did not like her hat, any more than he liked tropical flowers. It was the wrong hat for her, thought this Eastern businessman who had no interest whatever in women's clothes and no eye for them; he thought the unaccustomed thing crossly.

It must stick out all over me, she thought, so people think they can love me or hate me just by looking at me. How did it leave us—the old, safe, slow way people used to know of learning how one another feels, and the privilege that went with it of shying away if it seemed best? People in love like me, I suppose, give away the short cuts to everybody's secrets.

Something, though, he decided, had been settled about her predicament—for the time being, anyway; the parties to it were all still alive, no doubt. Nevertheless, her predicament was the only one he felt so sure of here, like the only recognizable shadow in that restaurant, where mirrors and fans were busy agitating the light, as the very local talk drawled across and agitated the peace. The shadow lay between her fingers, between her little square hand and her cheek, like something always best carried about the person. Then suddenly, as she took her hand down, the secret fact was still there—it lighted her. It was a bold and full light, shot up under the brim of that hat, as close to them all as the flowers in the center of the table.

Did he dream of making her disloyal to that hopelessness that he saw very well she'd been cultivating down here? He knew very well that he did not. What they amounted to was two Northerners keeping each other company. She glanced up at the big gold clock on the wall and smiled. He didn't smile back. She had that naive face that he associated, for no good reason, with the Middle West—because it said "Show me," perhaps. It was a serious, now-watch-out-everybody face, which orphaned her entirely in the company of these Southerners. He guessed her age, as he could not guess theirs: thirty-two. He himself was further along.

Of all human moods, deliberate imperviousness may be the most quickly communicated—it may be the most successful, most fatal signal of all. And two people can indulge in imperviousness as well as in anything else. "You're not very hungry either," he said.

The blades of fan shadows came down over their two heads, as he saw inadvertently in the mirror, with himself smiling at her now like a villain. His remark sounded dominant and rude enough for everybody present to listen back a moment; it even sounded like an answer to a question she might have just asked him. The other women glanced at him. The Southern look—Southern mask—of life-is-a-dream irony, which could turn to pure challenge at the drop of a hat, he could wish well away. He liked naïveté better.

"I find the heat down here depressing," she said, with the heart of Ohio in her voice.

"Well—I'm in somewhat of a temper about it, too," he said.

They looked with grateful dignity at each other.

"I have a car here, just down the street," he said to her as the luncheon party was rising to leave, all the others wanting to get back to their houses and sleep. "If it's all right with— Have you ever driven down south of here?"

Out on Bourbon Street, in the bath of July, she asked at his shoulder, "South of New Orleans? I didn't know there was any south to *here*. Does it just go on and on?" She laughed, and adjusted the exasperating hat to her head in a different way. It was more than frivolous, it was conspicuous, with some sort of glitter or flitter tied in a band around the straw and hanging down.

"That's what I'm going to show you."

"Oh—you've been there?"

"No!"

His voice rang out over the uneven, narrow sidewalk and dropped back from the walls. The flaked-off, colored houses were spotted like the hides of beasts faded and shy, and were hot as a wall of growth that seemed to breathe flower-like down onto them as they walked to the car parked there.

"It's just that it couldn't be any worse—we'll see."

"All right, then," she said. "We will."

So, their actions reduced to amiability, they settled into the car—a faded-red Ford convertible with a rather threadbare canvas top, which had been standing in the sun for all those lunch hours.

"It's rented," he explained. "I asked to have the top put down, and was told I'd lost my mind."

"It's out of this world. *Degrading* heat," she said and added, "Doesn't matter."

The stranger in New Orleans always sets out to leave it as though following the clue in a maze. They were threading through the narrow and one-way streets, past the pale-violet bloom of tired squares, the brown steeples and statues, the balcony with the live and probably famous black monkey dipping along the railing as over a ballroom floor, past the grillwork and the lattice-work to all the iron swans painted flesh color on the front steps of bungalows outlying.

Driving, he spread his new map and put his finger down on it. At the intersection marked Arabi, where their road led out of the tangle and he took it, a small Negro seated beneath a black umbrella astride a box chalked "Shou Shine" lifted his pink-and-black hand and waved them languidly good-by. She didn't miss it, and waved back.

Below New Orleans there was a raging of insects from both sides of the concrete highway, not quite together, like the playing of separated marching bands. The river and the levee were still on her side, waste and jungle and some occasional settlements on his—poor houses. Families bigger than housefuls thronged the yards. His nodding, driving head would veer from side to side, looking and almost lowering. As time passed and the distance from New Orleans grew, girls ever darker and younger were disposing themselves over the porches and the porch steps, with jet-black hair pulled high, and ragged palm-leaf fans rising and falling like rafts of butterflies. The children running forth were nearly always naked ones.

She watched the road. Crayfish constantly crossed in front of the wheels, looking grim and bonneted, in a great hurry.

"How the Old Woman Got Home," she murmured to herself.

He pointed, as it flew by, at a saucepan full of cut zinnias which stood waiting on the open lid of a mailbox at the roadside, with a little note tied onto the handle.

They rode mostly in silence. The sun bore down. They met fishermen and other men bent on some local pursuits, some in sulphur-colored pants, walking and riding; met wagons, trucks, boats in trucks, autos, boats on top of autos—all coming to meet them, as though something of high moment were doing back where the car came from, and he and she were determined to miss it. There was nearly always a man lying with his shoes off in the bed of any truck otherwise empty—with the raw, red look of a man sleeping in the daytime, being jolted about as he slept. Then there was a sort of dead man's land, where nobody came. He loosened his collar and tie. By rushing through the heat at high speed, they brought themselves the effect of fans turned onto their cheeks. Clearing alternated with jungle and canebrake like something tried,

tried again. Little shell roads led off on both sides; now and then a road of planks led into the yellow-green.

"Like a dance floor in there." She pointed.

He informed her, "In there's your oil, I think."

There were thousands, millions of mosquitoes and gnats —a universe of them, and on the increase.

A family of eight or nine people on foot strung along the road in the same direction the car was going, beating themselves with the wild palmettos. Heels, shoulders, knees, breasts, back of the heads, elbows, hands, were touched in turn—like some game, each playing it with himself.

He struck himself on the forehead, and increased their speed. (His wife would not be at her most charitable if he came bringing malaria home to the family.)

More and more crayfish and other shell creatures littered their path, scuttling or dragging. These little samples, little jokes of creation, persisted and sometimes perished, the more of them the deeper down the road went. Terrapins and turtles came up steadily over the horizons of the ditches.

Back there in the margins were worse—crawling hides you could not penetrate with bullets or quite believe, grins that had come down from the primeval mud.

"Wake up." Her Northern nudge was very timely on his arm. They had veered toward the side of the road. Still driving fast, he spread his map.

Like a misplaced sunrise, the light of the river flowed up; they were mounting the levee on a little shell road.

"Shall we cross here?" he asked politely.

He might have been keeping track over years and miles of how long they could keep that tiny ferry waiting. Now skidding down the levee's flank, they were the last-minute car, the last possible car that could squeeze on. Under the sparse shade of one willow tree, the small, amateurish-looking boat slapped the water, as, expertly, he wedged on board.

"Tell him we put him on hub cap!" shouted one of the numerous olive-skinned, dark-eyed young boys standing dressed up in bright shirts at the railing, hugging each other with delight that that last straw was on board. Another boy drew his affectionate initials in the dust of the door on her side.

She opened the door and stepped out, and, after only a moment's standing at bay, started up a little iron stairway. She appeared above the car, on the tiny bridge beneath the captain's window and the whistle.

From there, while the boat still delayed in what seemed a trance—as if it were too full to attempt the start—she could see the panlike deck below, separated by its rusty rim from the tilting, polished water.

The passengers walking and jostling about there appeared oddly amateurish, too—amateur travelers. They were having such a good time. They all knew each other. Beer was being passed around in cans, bets were being loudly settled and new bets made, about local and special subjects on which they all doted. One red-haired man in a burst of wildness even tried to give away his truckload of shrimp to a man on the other side of the boat—nearly all the trucks were full of shrimp—causing taunts and then protests of "They good! They good!" from the giver. The young boys leaned on each other thinking of what next, rolling their eyes absently.

A radio pricked the air behind her. Looking like a great tomcat just above her head, the captain was digesting the news of a fine stolen automobile.

At last a tremendous explosion burst—the whistle.

Everything shuddered in outline from the sound, everybody said something—everybody else.

They started with no perceptible motion, but her hat blew off. It went spiraling to the deck below, where he, thank heaven, sprang out of the car and picked it up. Everybody looked frankly up at her now, holding her hands to her head.

The little willow tree receded as its shade was taken away. The heat was like something falling on her head. She held the hot rail before her. It was like riding a stove. Her shoulders dropping, her hair flying, her skirt buffeted by the sudden strong wind, she stood there, thinking they all must see that with her entire self all she did was wait. Her set hands, with the bag that hung from her wrist and rocked back and forth—all three seemed objects bleaching there, belonging to no one; she could not feel a thing in the skin of her face; perhaps she was crying, and not knowing it. She could look down and see him just below her, his black shadow, her hat, and his black hair. His hair in the wind looked unreasonably long and rippling. Little did he know that from here it had a red undergleam like an animal's. When she looked up and outward, a vortex of light drove through and over the brown waves like a star in the water.

He did after all bring the retrieved hat up the stairs to her. She took it back—useless—and held it to her skirt. What they were saying below was more polite than their searchlight faces.

"Where you think he come from, that man?"

"I bet he come from Lafitte."

"Lafitte? What you bet, eh?"—all crouched in the shade of trucks, squatting and laughing.

Now his shadow fell partly across her; the boat had jolted into some other strand of current. Her shaded arm

and shaded hand felt pulled out from the blaze of light
and water, and she hoped humbly for more shade for her
head. It had seemed so natural to climb up and stand in
the sun.

The boys had a surprise—an alligator on board. One
of them pulled it by a chain around the deck, between
the cars and trucks, like a toy—a hide that could walk.
He thought, Well they had to catch one sometime. It's
Sunday afternoon. So they have him on board now, riding him across the Mississippi River. . . . The playful-
ness of it beset everybody on the ferry. The hoarseness
of the boat whistle, commenting briefly, seemed part of
the general appreciation.

"Who want to rassle him? Who want to, eh?" two boys
cried, looking up. A boy with shrimp-colored arms ca-
pered from side to side, pretending to have been bitten.

What was there so hilarious about jaws that could bite?
And what danger was there once in this repulsiveness—
so that the last worldly evidence of some old heroic horror
of the dragon had to be paraded in capture before the
eyes of country clowns?

He noticed that she looked at the alligator without
flinching at all. Her distance was set—the number of feet
and inches between herself and it mattered to her.

Perhaps her measuring coolness was to him what his
bodily shade was to her, while they stood pat up there
riding the river, which felt like the sea and looked like the
earth under them—full of the red-brown earth, charged
with it. Ahead of the boat it was like an exposed vein of
ore. The river seemed to swell in the vast middle with the
curve of the earth. The sun rolled under them. As if in
memory of the size of things, uprooted trees were drawn
across their path, sawing at the air and tumbling one
over the other.

When they reached the other side, they felt that they had been racing around an arena in their chariot, among lions. The whistle took and shook the stairs as they went down. The young boys, looking taller, had taken out colored combs and were combing their wet hair back in solemn pompadour above their radiant foreheads. They had been bathing in the river themselves not long before.

The cars and trucks, then the foot passengers and the alligator, waddling like a child to school, all disembarked and wound up the weed-sprung levee.

Both resp ctable and merciful, their hides, she thought, forcing herself to dwell on the alligator as she looked back. Deliver us all from the naked in heart. (As she had been told.)

When they regained their paved road, he heard her give a little sigh and saw her turn her straw-colored head to look back once more. Now that she rode with her hat in her lap, her earrings were conspicuous too. A little metal ball set with small pale stones danced beside each square, faintly downy cheek.

Had she felt a wish for someone else to be riding with them? He thought it was more likely that she would wish for her husband if she had one (his wife's voice) than for the lover in whom he believed. Whatever people liked to think, situations (if not scenes) were usually three-way —there was somebody else always. The one who didn't— couldn't—understand the two made the formidable third.

He glanced down at the map flapping on the seat between them, up at his wristwatch, out at the road. Out there was the incredible brightness of four o'clock.

On this side of the river, the road ran beneath the brow of the levee and followed it. Here was a heat that ran deeper and brighter and more intense than all the rest—its nerve. The road grew one with the heat as it was one with the unseen river. Dead snakes stretched across the concrete like markers—inlaid mosaic bands, dry as feathers, which their tires licked at intervals that began to seem clocklike.

No, the heat faced them—it was ahead. They could see it waving at them, shaken in the air above the white of the road, always at a certain distance ahead, shimmering finely as a cloth, with running edges of green and gold, fire and azure.

"It's never anything like this in Syracuse," he said.

"Or in Toledo, either," she replied with dry lips.

They were driving through greater waste down here, through fewer and even more insignificant towns. There was water under everything. Even where a screen of jungle had been left to stand, splashes could be heard from under the trees. In the vast open, sometimes boats moved inch by inch through what appeared endless meadows of rubbery flowers.

Her eyes overcome with brightness and size, she felt a panic rise, as sudden as nausea. Just how far below questions and answers, concealment and revelation, they were running now—that was still a new question, with a power of its own, waiting. How dear—how costly—could this ride be?

"It looks to me like your road can't go much further," she remarked cheerfully. "Just over there, it's all water."

"Time out," he said, and with that he turned the car into a sudden road of white shells that rushed at them narrowly out of the left.

They bolted over a cattle guard, where some rayed and crested purple flowers burst out of the vines in the ditch, and rolled onto a long, narrow, green, mowed clearing: a churchyard. A paved track ran between two short rows of raised tombs, all neatly white-washed and now brilliant as faces against the vast flushed sky.

The track was the width of the car with a few inches to spare. He passed between the tombs slowly but in the manner of a feat. Names took their places on the walls slowly at a level with the eye, names as near as the eyes of a person stopping in conversation, and as far away in origin, and in all their music and dead longing, as Spain. At intervals were set packed bouquets of zinnias, oleanders, and some kind of purple flowers, all quite fresh, in fruit jars, like nice welcomes on bureaus.

They moved on into an open plot beyond, of violent-green grass, spread before the green-and-white frame church with worked flower beds around it, flowerless poinsettias growing up to the windowsills. Beyond was a house, and left on the doorstep of the house a fresh-caught catfish the size of a baby—a fish wearing whiskers and bleeding. On a clothesline in the yard, a priest's black gown on a hanger hung airing, swaying at man's height, in a vague, trainlike, lady-like sweep along an evening breath that might otherwise have seemed imaginary from the unseen, felt river.

With the motor cut off, with the raging of the insects about them, they sat looking out at the green and white and black and red and pink as they leaned against the sides of the car.

"What is your wife like?" she asked. His right hand came up and spread—iron, wooden, manicured. She lifted her eyes to his face. He looked at her like that hand.

Then he lit a cigarette, and the portrait, and the right-hand testimonial it made, were blown away. She smiled, herself as unaffected as by some stage performance; and he was annoyed in the cemetery. They did not risk going on to her husband—if she had one.

Under the supporting posts of the priest's house, where a boat was, solid ground ended and palmettos and water hyacinths could not wait to begin; suddenly the rays of the sun, from behind the car, reached that lowness and struck the flowers. The priest came out onto the porch in his underwear, stared at the car a moment as if he wondered what time it was, then collected his robe off the line and his fish off the doorstep and returned inside. Vespers was next, for him.

After backing out between the tombs he drove on still south, in the sunset. They caught up with an old man walking in a sprightly way in their direction, all by himself, wearing a clean bright shirt printed with a pair of palm trees fanning green over his chest. It might better be a big colored woman's shirt, but she didn't have it. He flagged the car with gestures like hoops.

"You're coming to the end of the road," the old man told them. He pointed ahead, tipped his hat to the lady, and pointed again. "End of the road." They didn't understand that he meant, "Take me."

They drove on. "If we do go any further, it'll have to be by water—is that it?" he asked her, hesitating at this odd point.

"You know better than I do," she replied politely.

The road had for some time ceased to be paved; it was made of shells. It was leading into a small, sparse settlement like the others a few miles back, but with even more of the camp about it. On the lip of the clearing, directly before a green willow blaze with the sunset gone behind it, the row of houses and shacks faced out on broad, colored, moving water that stretched to reach the horizon and looked like an arm of the sea. The houses on their shaggy posts, patchily built, some with plank runways instead of steps, were flimsy and alike, and not much bigger than the boats tied up at the landing.

"Venice," she heard him announce, and he dropped the crackling map in her lap.

They coasted down the brief remainder. The end of the road—she could not remember ever seeing a road simply end—was a spoon shape, with a tree stump in the bowl to turn around by.

Around it, he stopped the car, and they stepped out, feeling put down in the midst of a sudden vast pause or subduement that was like a yawn. They made their way on foot toward the water, where at an idle-looking landing men in twos and threes stood with their backs to them.

The nearness of darkness, the still uncut trees, bright water partly under a sheet of flowers, shacks, silence, dark shapes of boats tied up, then the first sounds of people just on the other side of thin walls—all this reached them. Mounds of shells like day-old snow, pink-tinted, lay around a central shack with a beer sign on it. An old man up on the porch there sat holding an open newspaper, with a fat white goose sitting opposite him on the floor. Below, in the now shadowless and sunless open, another old man, with a colored pencil bright under his hat brim, was late mending a sail.

When she looked clear around, thinking they had a fire burning somewhere now, out of the heat had risen the full moon. Just beyond the trees, enormous, tangerine-colored, it was going solidly up. Other lights just striking into view, looking farther distant, showed moss shapes hanging, or slipped and broke matchlike on the water that so encroached upon the rim of ground they were standing on.

There was a touch at her arm—his, accidental.

"We're at the jumping-off place," he said.

She laughed, having thought his hand was a bat, while

her eyes rushed downward toward a great pale drift of
water hyacinths—still partly open, flushed and yet moon-
lit, level with her feet—through which paths of water for
the boats had been hacked. She drew her hands up to her
face under the brim of her hat; her own cheeks felt like
the hyacinths to her, all her skin still full of too much
light and sky, exposed. The harsh vesper bell was ringing.

"I believe there must be something wrong with me, that
I came on this excursion to begin with," she said, as if he
had already said this and she were merely in hopeful, willing, maddening agreement with him.

He took hold of her arm, and said, "Oh, come on—I
see we can get something to drink here, at least."

But there was a beating, muffled sound from over the
darkening water. One more boat was coming in, making
its way through the tenacious, tough, dark flower traps,
by the shaken light of what first appeared to be torches.
He and she waited for the boat, as if on each other's pa-
tience. As if borne in on a mist of twilight or a breath,
a horde of mosquitoes and gnats came singing and striking at them first. The boat bumped, men laughed. Somebody was offering somebody else some shrimp.

Then he might have cocked his dark city head down at
her; she did not look up at him, only turned when he did.
Now the shell mounds, like the shacks and trees, were solid
purple. Lights had appeared in the not-quite-true window
squares. A narrow neon sign, the lone sign, had come out
in bright blush on the beer shack's roof: "Baba's Place."
A light was on on the porch.

The barnlike interior was brightly lit and unpainted,
looking not quite finished, with a partition dividing this
room from what lay behind. One of the four cardplayers
at a table in the middle of the floor was the newspaper

reader; the paper was in his pants pocket. Midway along the partition was a bar, in the form of a pass-through to the other room, with a varnished, second-hand fretwork overhang. They crossed the floor and sat, alone there, on wooden stools. An eruption of humorous signs, newspaper cutouts and cartoons, razor-blade cards, and personal messages of significance to the owner or his friends decorated the overhang, framing where Baba should have been but wasn't.

Through there came a smell of garlic and cloves and red pepper, a blast of hot cloud escaped from a cauldron they could see now on a stove at the back of the other room. A massive back, presumably female, with a twist of gray hair on top, stood with a ladle akimbo. A young man joined her and with his fingers stole something out of the pot and ate it. At Baba's they were boiling shrimp.

When he got ready to wait on them, Baba strolled out to the counter, young, black-headed, and in very good humor.

"Coldest beer you've got. And food— What will you have?"

"Nothing for me, thank you," she said. "I'm not sure I could eat, after all."

"Well, I could," he said, shoving his jaw out. Baba smiled. "I want a good solid ham sandwich."

"I could have asked him for some water," she said, after he had gone.

While they sat waiting, it seemed very quiet. The bubbling of the shrimp, the distant laughing of Baba, and the slap of cards, like the beating of moths on the screens, seemed to come in fits and starts. The steady breathing they heard came from a big rough dog asleep in the corner. But it was bright. Electric lights were strung riotously over the room from a kind of spider web of old wires in the rafters. One of the written messages tacked before them read, "Joe! At the boyy!!" It looked very yellow, older than Baba's Place. Outside, the world was pure dark.

Two little boys, almost alike, almost the same size, and just cleaned up, dived into the room with a double bang of the screen door, and circled around the card game. They ran their hands into the men's pockets.

"Nickel for some pop!"

"Nickel for some pop!"

"Go 'way and let me play, you!"

They circled around and shrieked at the dog, ran under the lid of the counter and raced through the kitchen and back, and hung over the stools at the bar. One child had a live lizard on his shirt, clinging like a breast pin— like lapis lazuli.

Bringing in a strong odor of geranium talcum, some men had come in now—all in bright shirts. They drew near the counter, or stood and watched the game.

When Baba came out bringing the beer and sandwich, "Could I have some water?" she greeted him.

Baba laughed at everybody. She decided the woman back there must be Baba's mother.

Beside her, he was drinking his beer and eating his sandwich—ham, cheese, tomato, pickle, and mustard. Before he finished, one of the men who had come in beckoned from across the room. It was the old man in the palm-tree shirt.

She lifted her head to watch him leave her, and was looked at, from all over the room. As a minute passed, no cards were laid down. In a far-off way, like accepting the light from Arcturus, she accepted it that she was more beautiful or perhaps more fragile than the women they saw every day of their lives. It was just this thought coming into a woman's face, and at this hour, that seemed familiar to them.

Baba was smiling. He had set an opened, frosted brown

bottle before her on the counter, and a thick sandwich, and stood looking at her. Baba made her eat some supper, for what she was.

"What the old fellow wanted," said he when he came back at last, "was to have a friend of his apologize. Seems church is just out. Seems the friend made a remark coming in just now. His pals told him there was a lady present."

"I see you bought him a beer," she said.

"Well, the old man looked like he wanted *something*."

All at once the juke box interrupted from back in the corner, with the same old song as anywhere. The half-dozen slot machines along the wall were suddenly all run to like Maypoles, and thrown into action—taken over by further battalions of little boys.

There were three little boys to each slot machine. The local custom appeared to be that one pulled the lever for the friend he was holding up to put the nickel in, while the third covered the pictures with the flat of his hand as they fell into place, so as to surprise them all if anything happened.

The dog lay sleeping on in front of the raging juke box, his ribs working fast as a concertina's. At the side of the room a man with a cap on his white thatch was trying his best to open a side screen door, but it was stuck fast. It was he who had come in with the remark considered ribald; now he was trying to get out the other way. Moths as thick as ingots were trying to get in. The card players broke into shouts of derision, then joy, then tired derision among themselves; they might have been here all afternoon—they were the only ones not cleaned up and shaved. The original pair of little boys ran in once more, with the hyphenated bang. They got nickels this time, then were brushed away from the table like mosquitoes, and they rushed under the counter and on to the cauldron behind, clinging to Baba's mother there. The evening was at the threshold.

They were quite unnoticed now. He was eating another sandwich, and she, having finished part of hers, was fanning her face with her hat. Baba had lifted the flap of the counter and come out into the room. Behind his head there was a sign lettered in orange crayon: "Shrimp Dance Sun. PM." That was tonight, still to be.

And suddenly she made a move to slide down from her stool, maybe wishing to walk out into that nowhere down the front steps to be cool a moment. But he had hold of her hand. He got down from his stool, and, patiently, reversing her hand in his own—just as she had had the look of being about to give up, faint—began moving her, leading her. They were dancing.

"I get to thinking this is what we get—what you and I deserve," she whispered, looking past his shoulder into the room. "And all the time, it's real. It's a real place—away off down here . . ."

They danced gratefully, formally, to some song carried on in what must be the local patois, while no one paid any attention as long as they were together, and the children poured the family nickels steadily into the slot machines, walloping the handles down with regular crashes and troubling nobody with winning.

She said rapidly, as they began moving together too well, "One of those clippings was an account of a shooting right here. I guess they're proud of it. And that awful knife Baba was carrying . . . I wonder what he called me," she whispered in his ear.

"Who?"

"The one who apologized to you."

If they had ever been going to overstep themselves, it

would be now as he held her closer and turned her, when she became aware that he could not help but see the bruise at her temple. It would not be six inches from his eyes. She felt it come out like an evil star. (Let it pay him back, then, for the hand he had stuck in her face when she'd tried once to be sympathetic, when she'd asked about his wife.) They danced on still as the record changed, after standing wordless and motionless, linked together in the middle of the room, for the moment between.

Then, they were like a matched team—like professional, Spanish dancers wearing masks—while the slow piece was playing.

Surely even those immune from the world, for the time being, need the touch of one another, or all is lost. Their arms encircling each other, their bodies circling the odorous, just-nailed-down floor, they were, at last, imperviousness in motion. They had found it, and had almost missed it: they had had to dance. They were what their separate hearts desired that day, for themselves and each other.

They were so good together that once she looked up and half smiled. "For whose benefit did we have to show off?"

Like people in love, they had a superstition about themselves almost as soon as they came out on the floor, and dared not think the words "happy" or "unhappy," which might strike them, one or the other, like lightning.

In the thickening heat they danced on while Baba himself sang with the mosquito-voiced singer in the chorus of *"Moi pas l'aimez ça,"* enumerating the *ça's* with a hot shrimp between his fingers. He was counting over the platters the old woman now set out on the counter, each heaped with shrimp in their shells boiled to iridescence, like mounds of honeysuckle flowers.

The goose wandered in from the back room under the lid of the counter and hitched itself around the floor among the table legs and people's legs, never seeing that it was neatly avoided by two dancers—who nevertheless vaguely thought of this goose as learned, having earlier heard an old man read to it. The children called it Mimi, and lured it away. The old thatched man was again drunkenly trying to get out by the stuck side door; now he gave it a kick, but was prevailed on to remain. The sleeping dog shuddered and snored.

It was left up to the dancers to provide nickels for the juke box; Baba kept a drawerful for every use. They had grown fond of all the selections by now. This was the music you heard out of the distance at night—out of the roadside taverns you fled past, around the late corners in cities half asleep, drifting up from the carnival over the hill, with one odd little strain always managing to repeat itself. This seemed a homey place.

Bathed in sweat, and feeling the false coolness that brings, they stood finally on the porch in the lapping night air for a moment before leaving. The first arrivals of the girls were coming up the steps under the porch light—all flowered fronts, their black pompadours giving out breathlike feelers from sheer abundance. Where they'd resprinkled it since church, the talcum shone like mica on their downy arms. Smelling solidly of geranium, they filed across the porch with short steps and fingers joined, just timed to turn their smiles loose inside the room. He held the door open for them.

"Ready to go?" he asked her.

Going back, the ride was wordless, quiet except for the motor and the insects driving themselves against the car. The windshield was soon blinded. The headlights pulled in two other spinning storms, cones of flying things that, it seemed, might ignite at the last minute. He stopped the car and got out to clean the windshield thoroughly with his brisk, angry motions of driving. Dust lay thick and cratered on the roadside scrub. Under the now ash-white moon, the world traveled through very faint stars—very many slow stars, very high, very low.

It was a strange land, amphibious—and whether water-covered or grown with jungle or robbed entirely of water and trees, as now, it had the same loneliness. He regarded the great sweep—like steppes, like moors, like deserts (all of which were imaginary to him) ; but more than it was like any likeness, it was South. The vast, thin, wide-thrown, pale, unfocused star-sky, with its veils of light-ning adrift, hung over this land as it hung over the open sea. Standing out in the night alone, he was struck as powerfully with recognition of the extremity of this place as if all other bearings had vanished—as if snow had sud-denly started to fall.

He climbed back inside and drove. When he moved to slap furiously at his shirtsleeves, she shivered in the hot, licking night wind that their speed was making. Once the car lights picked out two people—a Negro couple, sitting on two facing chairs in the yard outside their lonely cabin —half undressed, each battling for self against the hot night, with long white rags in endless, scarflike motions.

In peopleless open places there were lakes of dust, smudge fires burning at their hearts. Cows stood in un-tended rings around them, motionless in the heat, in the night—their horns standing up sharp against that glow.

At length, he stopped the car again, and this time he put his arm under her shoulder and kissed her—not know-ing ever whether gently or harshly. It was the loss of that distinction that told him this was now. Then their faces touched unkissing, unmoving, dark, for a length of time. The heat came inside the car and wrapped them still, and the mosquitoes had begun to coat their arms and even their eyelids.

Later, crossing a large open distance, he saw at the same time two fires. He had the feeling that they had been riding for a long time across a face—great, wide, and upturned. In its eyes and open mouth were those fires they had had glimpses of, where the cattle had drawn together: a face, a head, far down here in the South—south of South, below it. A whole giant body sprawled downward then, on and on, always, constant as a constellation or an angel. Flaming and perhaps falling, he thought.

She appeared to be sound asleep, lying back flat as a child, with her hat in her lap. He drove on with her profile beside his, behind his, for he bent forward to drive faster. The earrings she wore twinkled with their rushing motion in an almost regular beat. They might have spoken like tongues. He looked straight before him and drove on, at a speed that, for the rented, overheated, not at all new Ford car, was demoniac.

It seemed often now that a barnlike shape flashed by, roof and all outlined in lonely neon—a movie house at a cross roads. The long white flat road itself, since they had followed it to the end and turned around to come back, seemed able, this far up, to pull them home.

A thing is incredible, if ever, only after it is told—returned to the world it came out of. For their different reasons, he thought, neither of them would tell this (unless something was dragged out of them) : that, strangers, they had ridden down into a strange land together and were getting safely back—by a slight margin, perhaps, but margin enough. Over the levee wall now, like an aurora borealis, the sky of New Orleans, across the river, was flickering gently. This time they crossed by bridge, high above everything, merging into a long light-stream of cars turned cityward.

For a time afterward he was lost in the streets, turning almost at random with the noisy traffic until he found his bearings. When he stopped the car at the next sign and leaned forward frowning to make it out, she sat up straight on her side. It was Arabi. He turned the car right around.

"We're all right now," he muttered, allowing himself a cigarette.

Something that must have been with them all along suddenly, then, was not. In a moment, tall as panic, it rose, cried like a human, and dropped back.

"I never got my water," she said.

She gave him the name of her hotel, he drove her there, and he said good night on the sidewalk. They shook hands.

"Forgive . . ." For, just in time, he saw she expected it of him.

And that was just what she did, forgive him. Indeed, had she waked in time from a deep sleep, she would have told him her story. She disappeared through the revolving door, with a gesture of smoothing her hair, and he thought a figure in the lobby strolled to meet her. He got back in the car and sat there.

He was not leaving for Syracuse until early in the morning. At length, he recalled the reason; his wife had recommended that he stay where he was this extra day so that she could entertain some old, unmarried college friends without him underfoot.

As he started up the car, he recognized in the smell of exhausted, body-warm air in the streets, in which the flow of drink was an inextricable part, the signal that the New Orleans evening was just beginning. In Dickie Grogan's, as he passed, the well-known Josefina at her organ was

charging up and down with *"Clair de Lune."* As he drove
the little Ford safely to its garage, he remembered for
the first time in years when he was young and brash, a
student in New York, and the shriek and horror and un-
holy smother of the subway had its original meaning for
him as the lilt and expectation of love.

The Burning

Delilah was dancing up to the front with a message; that was how she happened to be the one to see. A horse was coming in the house, by the front door. The door had been shoved wide open. And all behind the horse, a crowd with a long tail of dust was coming after, all the way up their road from the gate between the cedar trees.

She ran on into the parlor, where they were. They were standing up before the fireplace, their white sewing dropped over their feet, their backs turned, both ladies. Miss Theo had eyes in the back of her head.

"Back you go, Delilah," she said.

"It ain't me, it's them," cried Delilah, and now there were running feet to answer all over the downstairs; Ophelia and all had heard. Outside the dogs were thundering. Miss Theo and Miss Myra, keeping their backs turned to whatever shape or ghost Commotion would take when it came—as long as it was still in the yard, mounting the steps, crossing the porch, or even, with a smell of animal sudden as the smell of snake, planting itself in the front hall—they still had to see it if it came in the parlor, the white horse. It drew up just over the ledge of the double doors Delilah had pushed open, and the ladies lifted their heads together and looked in the mirror

28

over the fireplace, the one called the Venetian mirror, and there it was.

It was a white silhouette, like something cut out of the room's dark. July was so bright outside, and the parlor so dark for coolness, that at first nobody but Delilah could see. Then Miss Myra's racing speech interrupted everything.

"Will you take me on the horse? Please take me first."

It was a towering, sweating, grimacing, uneasy white horse. It had brought in two soldiers with red eyes and clawed, mosquito-racked faces—one a rider, hang-jawed and head-hanging, and the other walking by its side, all breathing in here now as loud as trumpets.

Miss Theo with shut eyes spoke just behind Miss Myra. "Delilah, what is it you came in your dirty apron to tell me?"

The sisters turned with linked hands and faced the room.

"Come to tell you we got the eggs away from black broody hen and sure enough, they's addled," said Delilah.

She saw the blue rider drop his jaw still lower. That was his laugh. But the other soldier set his boot on the carpet and heard the creak in the floor. As if reminded by tell-tale, he took another step, and with his red eyes sticking out he went as far as Miss Myra and took her around that little bending waist. Before he knew it, he had her lifted as high as a child, she was so light. The other soldier with a grunt came down from the horse's back and went toward Miss Theo.

"Step back, Delilah, out of harm's way," said Miss Theo, in such a company-voice that Delilah thought harm was one of two men.

"Hold my horse, nigger," said the man it was.

Delilah took the bridle as if she'd always done that, and held the horse that loomed there in the mirror—she could see it there now, herself—while more blurred and blindlike in the room between it and the door the first soldier shoved the tables and chairs out of the way behind Miss Myra, who flitted when she ran, and pushed her down where she stood and dropped on top of her. There in the mirror the parlor remained, filled up with dusted pictures, and shuttered since six o'clock against the heat and that smell of smoke they were all so tired of, still glimmering with precious, breakable things white ladies were never tired of and never broke, unless they were mad at each other. Behind *her*, the bare yawn of the hall was at her back, and the front stair's shadow, big as a tree and empty. Nobody went up there without being seen, and nobody was supposed to come down. Only if a cup or a silver spoon or a little string of spools on a blue ribbon came hopping down the steps like a frog, sometimes Delilah was the one to pick it up and run back up with it. Outside the mirror's frame, the flat of Miss Theo's hand came down on mankind with a boisterous sound.

Then Miss Theo lifted Miss Myra without speaking to her; Miss Myra closed her eyes but was not asleep. Her bands of black hair awry, her clothes rustling stiffly as clothes through winter quiet, Miss Theo strode half-carrying Miss Myra to the chair in the mirror, and put her down. It was the red, rubbed velvet, pretty chair like Miss Myra's ringbox. Miss Myra threw her head back, face up to the little plaster flowers going around the ceiling. She was asleep somewhere, if not in her eyes.

One of the men's voices spoke out, all gone with righteousness. "We just come in to inspect."

"You presume, you dare," said Miss Theo. Her hand

came down to stroke Miss Myra's back-flung head in a
strong, forbidding rhythm. From upstairs, Phinny threw
down his breakfast plate, but Delilah did not move. Miss
Myra's hair streamed loose behind her, bright gold, with
the combs caught like leaves in it. Maybe it was to keep
her like this, asleep in the heart, that Miss Theo stroked
her on and on, too hard.

"It's orders to inspect beforehand," said the soldier.

"Then inspect," said Miss Theo. "No man in the house
to prevent it. Brother—no word. Father—dead. Merci-
fully so—" She spoke in an almost rough-and-tumble kind
of way used by ladies who didn't like company—never did
like company, for anybody.

Phinny threw down his cup. The horse, shivering,
nudged Delilah who was holding him there, a good obe-
dient slave in her fresh-ironed candy-stripe dress beneath
her black apron. She would have had her turban tied on,
had she known all this ahead, like Miss Theo. "Never is
Phinny away. Phinny here. He a he," she said.

Miss Myra's face was turned up as if she were dead,
or as if she were a fierce and hungry little bird. Miss Theo
rested her hand for a moment in the air above her head.

"Is it shame that's stopping your inspection?" Miss
Theo asked. "I'm afraid you found the ladies of this
house a trifle out of your element. My sister's the more
delicate one, as you see. May I offer you this young
kitchen Negro, as I've always understood—"

That Northerner gave Miss Theo a serious, recording
look as though she had given away what day the mail
came in.

"My poor little sister," Miss Theo went on to Miss
Myra, "don't mind what you hear. Don't mind this old
world." But Miss Myra knocked back the stroking hand.

Kitty came picking her way into the room and sat between the horse's front feet; Friendly was her name.

One soldier rolled his head toward the other. "What was you saying to me when we come in, Virge?"

"I was saying I opined they wasn't gone yet."

"*Wasn't* they?"

Suddenly both of them laughed, jolting each other so hard that for a second it looked like a fight. Then one said with straight face, "We come with orders to set the house afire, ma'am," and the other one said, "General Sherman."

"I hear you."

"Don't you think we're going to do it? We done just burnt up Jackson twice," said the first soldier with his eye on Miss Myra. His voice made a man's big echo in the hall, like a long time ago. The horse whinnied and moved his head and feet.

"Like I was telling you, you ladies ought to been out. You didn't get no word here we was coming?" The other soldier pointed one finger at Miss Theo. She shut her eyes.

"Lady, they told you." Miss Myra's soldier looked hard at Miss Myra there. "And when your own people tell you something's coming to burn your house down, the business-like thing to do is get out of the way. And the right thing. I ain't beholden to tell you no more times now."

"Then go."

"Burning up *people's* further'n I go yet."

Miss Theo stared him down. "I see no degree."

So it was Miss Myra's soldier that jerked Delilah's hand from the bridle and turned her around, and cursed the Bedlam-like horse which began to beat the hall floor behind. Delilah listened, but Phinny did not throw anything more down; maybe he had crept to the landing, and

now looked over. He was scared, if not of horses, then of
men. He didn't know anything about them. The horse did
get loose; he took a clattering trip through the hall and
dining room and library, until at last his rider caught
him. Then Delilah was set on his back.

She looked back over her shoulder through the doorway, and saw Miss Theo shake Miss Myra and catch the
peaked face with its purple eyes and slap it.

"Myra," she said, "collect your senses. We have to go
out in front of them."

Miss Myra slowly lifted her white arm, like a lady who
has been asked to dance, and called, "Delilah!" Because
that was the one she saw being lifted onto the horse's hilly
back and ridden off through the front door. Skittering
among the iron shoes, Kitty came after, trotting fast as
a little horse herself, and ran ahead to the woods, where
she was never seen again; but Delilah, from where she was
set up on the horse and then dragged down on the grass,
never called after her.

She might have been saving her breath for the screams
that soon took over the outdoors and circled that house
they were going to finish for sure now. She screamed,
young and strong, for them all—for everybody that
wanted her to scream for them, for everybody that didn't;
and sometimes it seemed to her that she was screaming
her loudest for Delilah, who was lost now—carried out of
the house, not knowing how to get back.

Still inside, the ladies kept them waiting.

Miss Theo finally brought Miss Myra out through that
wide-open front door and across the porch with the still
perfect and motionless vine shadows. There were some cat-
calls and owl hoots from under the trees.

"Now hold back, boys. They's too lady-like for you."

"Ladies must needs take their time."

"And then they're no damn good at it!" came a clear, youthful voice, and under the branches somewhere a banjo was stroked to call up the campfires further on, later in the evening, when all this would be over and done.

The sisters showed no surprise to see soldiers and Negroes alike (old Ophelia in the way, talking, talking) strike into and out of the doors of the house, the front now the same as the back, to carry off beds, tables, candlesticks, washstands, cedar buckets, china pitchers, with their backs bent double; or the horses ready to go; or the food of the kitchen bolted down—and so much of it thrown away, this must be a second dinner; or the unsilenceable dogs, the old pack mixed with the strangers and fighting with all their hearts over bones. The last skinny sacks were thrown on the wagons—the last flour, the last scraping and clearing from Ophelia's shelves, even her pepper-grinder. The silver Delilah could count was counted on strange blankets and then, knocking against the teapot, rolled together, tied up like a bag of bones. A drummer boy with his drum around his neck caught both Miss Theo's peacocks, Marco and Polo, and wrung their necks in the yard. Nobody could look at those bird-corpses; nobody did.

The sisters left the porch like one, and in step, hands linked, came through the high grass in their crushed and only dresses, and walked under the trees. They came to a stop as if it was moonlight under the leafy frame of the big tree with the swing, without any despising left in their faces which were the same as one, as one face that didn't belong to anybody. This one clarified face, looking both left and right, could make out every one of those men through the bushes and tree trunks, and mark every

looting slave also, as all stood momently fixed like sere-
naders by the light of a moon. Only old Ophelia was talking all the time, all the time, telling everybody in her own
way about the trouble here, but of course nobody could
understand a thing that day anywhere in the world.

"What are they fixing to do now, Theo?" asked Miss
Myra, with a frown about to burn into her too-white forehead.

"What they want to," Miss Theo said, folding her arms.

To Delilah that house they were carrying the torches
to was like one just now coming into being—like the show-
boat that slowly came through the trees just once in her
time, at the peak of high water—bursting with the unknown, sparking in ruddy light, with a minute to go before that ear-aching cry of the calliope.

When it came—but it was a bellowing like a bull, that
came from inside—Delilah drew close, with Miss Theo's
skirt to peep around, and Miss Theo's face looked down
like death itself and said, "Remember this. You black
monkeys," as the blaze outdid them all.

A while after the burning, when everybody had gone
away, Miss Theo and Miss Myra, finding and taking hold
of Delilah who was face-down in a ditch with her eyes
scorched open, did at last go beyond the tramped-down
gate and away through the grand worthless fields they
themselves had had burned long before.

It was a hot afternoon, hot out here in the open, and
it played a trick on them with a smell and prophecy of
fall—it was the burning. The brown wet standing among
the stumps in the cracked cup of the pond tasted as hot
as coffee and as bitter. There was still and always smoke
between them and the sun.

After all the July miles, there Jackson stood, burned twice, or who knew if it was a hundred times, facing them in the road. Delilah could see through Jackson like a haunt, it was all chimneys, all scooped out. There were soldiers with guns among the ashes, but these ashes were cold. Soon even these two ladies, who had been everywhere and once knew their way, told each other they were lost. While some soldiers looked them over, they pointed at what they couldn't see, traced gone-away spires, while a horse without his rider passed brushing his side against them and ran down a black alley softly, and did not return.

They walked here and there, sometimes over the same track, holding hands all three, like the timeless time it snowed, and white and black went to play together in hushed woods. They turned loose only to point and name.

"The State House."—"The school."

"The Blind School."—"The penintentiary!"

"The big stable."—"The Deaf-and-Dumb."

"Oh! Remember when we passed three of *them*, sitting on a hill?" They went on matching each other, naming and claiming ruin for ruin.

"The lunatic asylum!"—"The State House."

"No, I said that. Now where are we? That's surely Captain Jack Calloway's hitching post."

"But why would the hitching post be standing and the rest not?"

"And ours not."

"I think I should have told you, Myra—"

"Tell me now."

"Word *was* sent to us to get out when it was sent to the rest on Vicksburg Road. Two days' warning. I believe it was a message from General Pemberton."

"Don't worry about it now. Oh no, of course we couldn't

leave," said Miss Myra. A soldier watched her in the distance, and she recited:

> "There was a man in our town
> And he was wondrous wise.
> He jumped into a bramble bush
> And scratched out both his eyes."

She stopped, looking at the soldier.

"He sent word," Miss Theo went on, "General Pemberton sent word, for us all to get out ahead of what was coming. You were in the summerhouse when it came. It was two days' warning—but I couldn't bring myself to call and tell you, Myra. I suppose I couldn't convince myself—couldn't quite *believe* that they meant to come and visit that destruction on us."

"Poor Theo. I could have."

"No you couldn't. I couldn't *understand* that message, any more than Delilah here could have. I can reproach myself now, of course, with everything." And they began to walk boldly through and boldly out of the burnt town, single file.

"Not everything, Theo. Who had Phinny? Remember?" cried Miss Myra ardently.

"Hush."

"If I hadn't had Phinny, that would've made it all right. Then Phinny wouldn't have—"

"Hush, dearest, that wasn't *your* baby, you know. It was Brother Benton's baby. I won't have your nonsense now." Miss Theo led the way through the ashes, marching in front. Delilah was in danger of getting left behind.

"—perished. Dear Benton. So good. Nobody else would have felt so *bound*," Miss Myra said.

"Not after I told him what he owed a little life! Each

little life is a *man's* fault, I said that. Oh, who'll ever forget that awful day?"

"Benton's forgotten, if he's dead. He was so good after that too, never married."

"Stayed home, took care of his sisters. Only wanted to be forgiven."

"There has to be somebody to take care of everybody."

"I told him, he must never dream he was *inflicting* his sisters. That's what we're for."

"And it never would have inflicted us. We could have lived and died. Until *they* came."

"In at the front door on the back of a horse," said Miss Theo. "If Benton had been there!"

"I'll never know what possessed them, riding in like that," said Miss Myra almost mischievously; and Miss Theo turned.

"And *you said*—"

"I said something wrong," said Miss Myra quickly. "I apologize, Theo."

"No, I blame only myself. That I let you remain one hour in that house after it was doomed. I thought I was equal to it, and I proved I was, but not you."

"Oh, to my shame you saw me, dear! Why do you say it wasn't my baby?"

"Now don't start that nonsense over again," said Miss Theo, going around a hole.

"I had Phinny. When we were all at home and happy together. Are you going to take Phinny away from me now?"

Miss Theo pressed her cheeks with her palms and showed her pressed, pensive smile as she looked back over her shoulder.

Miss Myra said, "Oh, don't *I* know who it really belonged to, who it loved the best, that baby?"

"I won't have you misrepresenting yourself."

"It's never what I intended."

"Then reason dictates you hush."

Both ladies sighed, and so did Delilah; they were so tired of going on. Miss Theo still walked in front but she was looking behind her through the eyes in the back of her head.

"You hide him if you want to," said Miss Myra. "Let Papa shut up all upstairs. I had him, dear. It was an officer, no, one of our beaux that used to come out and hunt with Benton. It's because I was always the impetuous one, highstrung and so easily carried away . . . And if Phinny *was* mine—"

"Don't you know he's black?" Miss Theo blocked the path.

"He *was* white." Then, "He's black *now*," whispered Miss Myra, darting forward and taking her sister's hands. Their shoulders were pressed together, as if they were laughing or waiting for something more to fall.

"If I only had something to eat!" sobbed Miss Myra, and once more let herself be embraced. One eye showed over the tall shoulder. "Oh, Delilah!"

"Could be he got out," called Delilah in a high voice. "He strong, he."

"Who?"

"Could be Phinny's out loose. Don't cry."

"Look yonder. What do I see? I see the Dicksons' perfectly good hammock still under the old pecan trees," Miss Theo said to Miss Myra, and spread her hand.

There was some little round silver cup, familiar to the ladies, in the hammock when they came to it down in the grove. Lying on its side with a few drops in it, it made them smile.

The yard was charged with butterflies. Miss Myra, as if she could wait no longer, climbed into the hammock and lay down with ankles crossed. She took up the cup like a story book she'd begun and left there yesterday, holding it before her eyes in those freckling fingers, slowly picking out the ants.

"So still out here and all," Miss Myra said. "Such a big sky. Can you get used to that? And all the figs dried up. I wish it would rain."

"Won't rain till Saturday," said Delilah.

"Delilah, don't go 'way."

"Don't you try, Delilah," said Miss Theo.

"No'm."

Miss Theo sat down, rested a while, though she did not know how to sit on the ground and was afraid of grasshoppers, and then she stood up, shook out her skirt, and cried out to Delilah, who had backed off far to one side, where some chickens were running around loose with nobody to catch them.

"Come back here, Delilah! Too late for that!" She said to Miss Myra, "The Lord will provide. We've still got Delilah, and as long as we've got her we'll use her, my dearie."

Miss Myra "let the cat die" in the hammock. Then she gave her hand to climb out, Miss Theo helped her, and without needing any help for herself Miss Theo untied the hammock from the pecan trees. She was long bent over it, and Miss Myra studied the butterflies. She had left the cup sitting on the ground in the shade of the tree. At last Miss Theo held up two lengths of cotton rope, the red and the white strands untwisted from each other, bent like the hair of ladies taken out of plaits in the morning.

Delilah, given the signal, darted up the tree and hooking her toes made the ropes fast to the two branches a

sociable distance apart, where Miss Theo pointed. When
she slid down, she stood waiting while they settled it, until
Miss Myra repeated enough times, in a spoiled sweet way,
"I bid to be first." It was what Miss Theo wanted all the
time. Then Delilah had to squat and make a basket with
her fingers, and Miss Myra tucked up her skirts and
stepped her ashy shoe in the black hands.

"Tuck under, Delilah."

Miss Myra, who had ordered that, stepped over Delilah's head and stood on her back, and Delilah felt her
presence tugging there as intimately as a fish's on a line,
each longing Miss Myra had to draw away from Miss
Theo, draw away from Delilah, away from that tree.

Delilah rolled her eyes around. The noose was being
tied by Miss Theo's puckered hands like a bonnet on a
windy day, and Miss Myra's young, lifted face was looking out.

"I learned as a child how to tie, from a picture book
in Papa's library—not that I ever was called on," Miss
Theo said. "I guess I was always something of a tomboy." She kissed Miss Myra's hand and at almost the
same instant Delilah was seized by the ribs and dragged
giggling backwards, out from under—not soon enough,
for Miss Myra kicked her in the head—a bad kick, almost as if that were Miss Theo or a man up in the tree,
who meant what he was doing.

Miss Theo stood holding Delilah and looking up—help-
ing herself to grief. No wonder Miss Myra used to hide
in the summerhouse with her reading, screaming sometimes when there was nothing but Delilah throwing the
dishwater out on the ground.

"I've proved," said Miss Theo to Delilah, dragging her
by more than main force back to the tree, "what I've always suspicioned: that I'm brave as a lion. That's right:

look at me. If I ordered you back up that tree to help my sister down to the grass and shade, you'd turn and run: I know your minds. You'd desert me with your work half done. So I haven't said a word about it. About mercy. As soon as you're through, you can go, and leave us where you've put us, unspared, just alike. And that's the way they'll find us. The sight will be good for them for what they've done," and she pushed Delilah down and walked up on her shoulders, weighting her down like a rock.

Miss Theo looped her own knot up there; there was no mirror or sister to guide her. Yet she was quicker this time than last time, but Delilah was quicker too. She rolled over in a ball, and then she was up running, looking backward, crying. Behind her Miss Theo came sailing down from the tree. She was always too powerful for a lady. Even those hens went flying up with a shriek, as if they felt her shadow on their backs. Now she reached in the grass.

There was nothing for Delilah to do but hide, down in the jungly grass choked with bitterweed and black-eyed susans, wild to the pricking skin, with many heads nodding, cauldrons of ants, with butterflies riding them, grasshoppers hopping them, mosquitoes making the air alive, down in the loud and lonesome grass that was rank enough almost to matt the sky over. Once, stung all over and wild to her hair's ends, she ran back and asked Miss Theo, "What must I do now? Where must I go?" But Miss Theo, whose eyes from the ground were looking straight up at her, wouldn't tell. Delilah danced away from her, back to her distance and crouched down. She believed Miss Theo twisted in the grass like a dead snake until the sun went down. She herself held still like a mantis until the grass had folded and spread apart at the falling of dew. This was after the chickens had gone to roost in a strange un-

easy tree against the cloud where the guns still boomed
and the way from Vicksburg was red. Then Delilah could
find her feet.

She knew where Miss Theo was. She could see the last
white of Miss Myra, the stockings. Later, down by the
swamp, in a wading bird tucked in its wing for sleep, she
saw Miss Myra's ghost.

After being lost a day and a night or more, crouching awhile, stealing awhile through the solitudes of briar
bushes, she came again to Rose Hill. She knew it by the
chimneys and by the crape myrtle off to the side, where
the bottom of the summerhouse stood empty as an egg
basket. Some of the flowers looked tasty, like chicken legs
fried a little black.

Going around the house, climbing over the barrier of
the stepless back doorsill, and wading into ashes, she was
lost still, inside that house. She found an iron pot and a
man's long boot, a doorknob and a little book flutter-
ing, its leaves spotted and fluffed like guinea feathers.
She took up the book and read out from it, "Ba-ba-ba-
ba-ba—trash." She was being Miss Theo taking away
Miss Myra's reading. Then she saw the Venetian mirror
down in the chimney's craw, flat and face-up in the cin-
ders.

Behind her the one standing wall of the house held
notched and listening like the big ear of King Solomon
into which poured the repeated asking of birds. The tree
stood and flowered. What must she do? Crouching suddenly to the ground, she heard the solid cannon, the gal-
loping, the low fast drum of burning. Crawling on her
knees she went to the glass and rubbed it with spit and
leaned over it and saw a face all neck and ears, then gone.
Before it she opened and spread her arms; she had seen

Miss Myra do that, try that. But its gleam was addled.

Though the mirror did not know Delilah, Delilah would have known that mirror anywhere, because it was set between black men. Their arms were raised to hold up the mirror's roof, which now the swollen mirror brimmed, among gold leaves and gold heads—black men dressed in gold, looking almost into the glass themselves, as if to look back through a door, men now half-split away, flattened with fire, bearded, noseless as the moss that hung from swamp trees.

Where the mirror did not cloud like the horse-trampled spring, gold gathered itself from the winding water, and honey under water started to flow, and then the gold fields were there, hardening gold. Through the water, gold and honey twisted up into houses, trembling. She saw people walking the bridges in early light with hives of houses on their heads, men in dresses, some with red birds; and monkeys in velvet; and ladies with masks laid over their faces looking from pointed windows. Delilah supposed that was Jackson before Sherman came. Then it was gone. In this noon quiet, here where all had passed by, unless indeed it had gone in, she waited on her knees.

The mirror's cloudy bottom sent up minnows of light to the brim where now a face pure as a water-lily shadow was floating. Almost too small and deep down to see, they were quivering, leaping to life, fighting, aping old things Delilah had seen done in this world already, sometimes what men had done to Miss Theo and Miss Myra and the peacocks and to slaves, and sometimes what a slave had done and what anybody now could do to anybody. Under the flicker of the sun's licks, then under its whole blow and blare, like an unheard scream, like an act of mercy gone, as the wall-less light and July blaze struck through from the opened sky, the mirror felled her flat.

She put her arms over her head and waited, for they would all be coming again, gathering under her and above her, bees saddled like horses out of the air, butterflies harnessed to one another, bats with masks on, birds together, all with their weapons bared. She listened for the blows, and dreaded that whole army of wings—of flies, birds, serpents, their glowing enemy faces and bright kings' dresses, that banner of colors forked out, all this world that was flying, striking, stricken, falling, gilded or blackened, mortally splitting and falling apart, proud turbans unwinding, turning like the spotted dying leaves of fall, spiraling down to bottomless ash; she dreaded the fury of all the butterflies and dragonflies in the world riding, blades unconcealed and at point—descending, and rising again from the waters below, down under, one whale made of his own grave, opening his mouth to swallow Jonah one more time.

Jonah!—a homely face to her, that could still look back from the red lane he'd gone down, even if it was too late to speak. He was her Jonah, her Phinny, her black monkey; she worshiped him still, though it was long ago he was taken from her the first time.

Stiffly, Delilah got to her feet. She cocked her head, looked sharp into the mirror, and caught the motherly image—head wagging in the flayed forehead of a horse with ears and crest up stiff, the shield and the drum of big swamp birdskins, the horns of deer sharpened to cut and kill with. She showed her teeth. Then she looked in the feathery ashes and found Phinny's bones. She ripped a square from her manifold fullness of skirts and tied up the bones in it.

She set foot in the road then, walking stilted in Miss Myra's shoes and carrying Miss Theo's shoes tied together around her neck, her train in the road behind her. She

wore Miss Myra's willing rings—had filled up two fingers
—but she had had at last to give up the puzzle of Miss
Theo's bracelet with the chain. They were two stones now,
scalding-white. When the combs were being lifted from her
hair, Miss Myra had come down too, beside her sister.

Light on Delilah's head the Jubilee cup was set. She
paused now and then to lick the rim and taste again the
ghost of sweet that could still make her tongue start clinging—some sweet lapped up greedily long ago, only a mystery now when or who by. She carried her own black lo-
cust stick to drive the snakes.

Following the smell of horses and fire, to men, she kept
in the wheel tracks till they broke down at the river. In
the shade underneath the burned and fallen bridge she sat
on a stump and chewed for a while, without dreams, the
comb of a dirtdauber. Then once more kneeling, she took
a drink from the Big Black, and pulled the shoes off her
feet and waded in.

Submerged to the waist, to the breast, stretching her
throat like a sunflower stalk above the river's opaque skin,
she kept on, her treasure stacked on the roof of her head,
hands laced upon it. She had forgotten how or when she
knew, and she did not know what day this was, but she
knew—it would not rain, the river would not rise, until
Saturday.

The Bride of the Innisfallen

There was something of the pavilion about one raincoat, the way—for some little time out there in the crowd—it stood flowing in its salmony-pink and yellow stripes down toward the wet floor of the platform, expanding as it went. In the Paddington gloom it was a little dim, but it was parading through now, and once inside the compartment it looked rainbow-bright.

In it a middle-aged lady climbed on like a sheltered girl —a boost up from behind she pretended not to need or notice. She was big-boned and taller than the man who followed her inside bringing the suitcase—he came up round and with a doll's smile, his black suit wet; she turned a look on him; this was farewell. The train to Fishguard to catch the Cork boat was leaving in fifteen minutes—at a black four o'clock in the afternoon of that spring that refused to flower. She, so clearly, was the one going.

There was nobody to share the compartment yet but one girl, and she not Irish.

Over a stronghold of a face, the blue hat of the lady in the raincoat was settled on like an Indian bonnet, or, rather, like an old hat, which it was. The hair that had been pulled out of its confines was flirtatious and went into two auburn-and-gray pomegranates along her cheeks.

Her gaze was almost forgiving, if unsettled; it held its shine so long. Even yet, somewhere, sometime, the owner of those eyes might expect to rise to a tragic occasion. When the round man put the suitcase up in the rack, she sank down under it as if something were now done that could not be undone, and with tender glances brushed the soot and raindrops off herself, somewhat onto him. He perched beside her—it was his legs that were short—and then, as her hands dropped into her bright-stained lap, they both stared straight ahead, as if waiting for a metamorphosis.

The American girl sitting opposite could not have taken in anything they said as long as she kept feeling it necessary, herself, to subside. As long as the train stood in the station, her whole predicament seemed betrayed by her earliness. She was leaving London without her husband's knowledge. She was wearing rather worn American clothes and thin shoes, and, sitting up very straight, kept pulling her coat collar about her ears and throat. In the strange, diminished light of the station people seemed to stand and move on some dark stage; by now platform and train must be almost entirely Irish in their gathered population.

A fourth person suddenly came inside the compartment, a small, passionate-looking man. He was with them as suddenly as a gift—as if an arm had thrust in a bunch of roses or a telegram. There seemed something in him about to explode, but—he pushed off his wet coat, threw it down, threw it up overhead, flung himself into the seat—he was going to be a good boy.

"What's the time?" The round man spoke softly, as if perhaps the new man had brought it.

The lady bowed her head and looked up at him: *she* had

it: "Six minutes to four." She wore an accurate-looking
wristwatch.

The round man's black eyes flared, he looked out at the
rain, and asked the American if she, too, were going to
Cork—a question she did not at first understand; his voice
was very musical.

"Yes—that is—"

"Four minutes to four," the lady in the raincoat said,
those fours sounding fated.

"You don't need to get out of the carriage till you get
to Fishguard," the round man told her, murmuring it
softly, as if he'd told her before and would tell her again.
"Straight through to Fishguard, then you book a berth.
You're in Cork in the morning."

She looked fondly as though she had never heard of
Cork, wouldn't believe it, and opened and shut her great
white heavy eyelids. When he crossed his knees she stole
her arm through his and seesawed him on the seat. Holding his rows of little black-rimmed fingers together like a
modest accordion, he said, "Two ladies going to Cork."

"Two minutes to four," she said, rolling her eyes.

"You'll go through the customs when you get to Fishguard," he told her. "They'll open your case and see what
there is to detect. They'll be wanting to discover if you
are bringing anything wrongly and improperly into the
country." He eyed the lady, above their linked arms, as
if she had been a stranger inquiring into the uses and
purposes of customs inspection in the world. By ceasing
to smile he appeared to anchor himself; he said solidly,
"Following that, you go on board."

"Where you won't be able to buy drink for three miles
out!" cried the new passenger. Up to now he had been
simply drawing quick breaths. He had a neat, short, tender, slightly alarmed profile—dark, straight hair cut not

ten minutes ago, a slight cut over the ear. But this still-bleeding customer, a Connemara man as he was now announcing himself, always did everything last-minute, because that was the way he was made.

There was a feel of the train's being about to leave. Then the guard was shouting.

The round man and the lady in the raincoat rose and moved in step to the door together, all four hands enjoined. She bent her head. Hers was a hat of drapes and shapes. There in the rainy light it showed a chaos of blue veil falling behind, and when it sadly turned, shining directly over the eyes was a gold pin in the shape of a pair of links, like those you are supposed to separate in amateur-magician sets. Her raincoat gave off a peppermint smell that might have been stored up for this moment.

"You won't need to get out of the carriage at all," he said. She put her head on one side. Their cheeks glittered as did their eyes. They embraced, parted; the man from Connemara watched him out the door. Then the pair clasped hands through the window. She might have been standing in a tower and he elevated to her level as far as possible by ladder or rope, in the rain.

There was a great rush of people. At the very last minute four of them stormed this compartment. A little boy flung in over his own bags, whistling wildly, paying no attention to being seen off, no attention to feet inside, consenting to let a young woman who had followed him in put a small bag of his in the rack and save him a seat. She was being pelted with thanks for this by young men and girls crowding at the door; she smiled calmly back at them; even in this she was showing pregnancy, as she showed it under her calm blue coat. A pair of lovers slid in last of all, like a shadow, and filled two seats by the corridor door, trapping into the middle the man from Con-

nemara and somewhat crowding the American girl into her
corner. They were just not twining, touching, just not
angry, just not too late. Without the ghost of impatience
or struggle, without shifting about once, they were settled
in speechlessness—two profiles, his dark and cleared of
temper, hers young, with straight cut hair.

"Four o'clock."

The lady in the raincoat made the announcement in a
hollow tone; everybody in the compartment hushed as
though almost taken by surprise. She and the wistful
round man still clasped hands through the window and
continued to shine in the face like lighthouses smiling.
The outside doors were banged shut in a long retreat in
both directions, and the train moved. Those outside appeared running beside the train, then waving handkerchiefs, the young men shouting questions and envious
things, the girls—they were certainly all Irish, wildly
pretty—wildly retreating, their hair whipped forward in
long bright and dark pennants by the sucking of the
train. The round little man was there one moment and,
panting, vanished the next.

The lady, still standing, was all at once very notice-
able. Her body might have solidified to the floor under
that buttoned cover. (What she had on under her raincoat was her own business and remained so.) The next
moment she put out her tongue, at everything just left
behind.

"*Oh* my God!" The man from Connemara did explode;
it sounded like relief.

Then they were underway fast; the lady, having seated
herself, smoothed down the raincoat with rattles like the
reckless slamming of bureau drawers, and took from her
purse a box of Players. She extracted a cigarette already

partly burned down, and requested a light. The lover was so quick he almost anticipated her. When the butt glowed, her hand dropped like a shot bird from the flame he rather blindly stuck out. Between draws she held her cigarette below her knees and turned inward to her palm—her hand making a cauldron into which the little boy stared.

The American girl opened a book, but closed it. Every time the lady in the raincoat walked out over their feet —she immediately, after her cigarette, made several excursions—she would fling them a look. It was like "Don't say a word, start anything, fall into each other's arms, read, or fight, until I get back to you." She might both inspire and tantalize them with her glare. And she was so unpretty she ought to be funny, like somebody on the stage; perhaps she would be funny later.

The little boy whistled *"Funiculi, Funicula"* in notes almost too high for the ear to hear. On the windows it poured, poured rain. The black of London swam like a cinder in the eye and did not go away. The young wife, leaning back and letting her eyes fall a little while on the child, gave him dim, languorous looks, not quite shaking her head at him. He stopped whistling, but at the same time it could be felt how she was not his mother; her face showed degrees of maternity as other faces show degrees of love or anger; she was only acting his mother for the journey.

It was nice of her then to begin to sing *"Funiculi, Funicula,"* and the others joined, the little boy very seriously, as if he now hated the song. Then they sang something more Irish, about the sea and coming back. But the throb of the rails made the song oddly Spanish and hopelessly desirous; they were near the end of the car, where the beat was single and strong.

After the lady in the raincoat undid her top button

and suggested "Wild Colonial Boy," her hatted head kept time, started to lead them—perhaps she kept a pub. The little boy, giving the ladies a meeting look, brought out a fiercely shining harmonica, as he would a pistol, and almost drowned them out. The American girl looked as if she did not know the words, but the lovers now sang, with faces strangely brave.

At some small, forgotten station a schoolgirl got on, took the vacant seat in this compartment, and opened a novel to page 1. They quieted. By the look of her it seemed they must be in Wales. They had scarcely got a word at the child before she began reading. She sat by the young wife; especially from her, the school hat hid the bent head like a candle snuffer; of her features only the little mouth, slightly open and working, stayed visible. Even her upper lip was darkly freckled, even the finger that lifted and turned the page.

The little boy sped his breath up the harmonica scale; the young wife said "Victor!" and they all felt sorry for him and had his name.

"Air," she suddenly said, as if she felt their look. The man from Connemara hurled himself at the window and slid the pane, then at the corridor door, and opened it wide onto a woman passing with an eight- or nine-months-old baby. It was a red-haired boy with queenly jowls, squinting in at the world as if to say, "Will what has just been said be very kindly repeated?"

"Oh, isn't he *beautiful!*" the young wife cried reproachfully through the door. She would have put out her hands.

There was no response. On they went.

"An English nurse traveling with an Irish child, look at that, he's so grand, and such style, that dress, that petticoat, do you think she's kidnaped the lad?" suggested the lady in the raincoat, puffing.

"*Oh* my God," said the man from Connemara.

For a moment the schoolgirl made the only sounds—catching her breath and sobbing over her book.

"Kidnaping's farfetched," said the man from Connemara. "Maybe the woman's deaf and dumb."

"I couldn't sleep this night thinking such wickedness was traveling on the train and on the boat with me." The young wife's skin flooded to her temples.

"It's not *your* fault."

The schoolgirl bent lower still and, still reading, opened a canvas satchel at her feet, in which—all looked—were a thermos, a lunchbox under lock and key, a banana, and a Bible. She selected the banana by feel, and brought it up and ate it as she read.

"If it's kidnaping, it'll be in the Cork paper Sunday morning," said the lady in the raincoat with confidence. "Railway trains are great systems for goings on of all kinds. You'll never take me by surprise."

"But this is *our* train," said the young wife. "Women alone, sometimes exceptions, but often on the long journey alone or with children."

"There's evil where you'd least expect it," the man from Connemara said, somehow as if he didn't care for children. "There's one thing and another, so forth and so on, run your finger down the alphabet and see where it stops."

"I'll never see the Cork paper," replied the young wife. "But oh, I tell you I would rather do without air to breathe than see that poor baby pass again and put out his little arms to me."

"Ah, then. Shut the door," the man from Connemara said, and pointed it out to the lover, who after all sat nearer.

"Excuse me," the young man whispered to the girl, and shut the door at her knee and near where her small open hand rested.

"But why would she be kidnaping the baby *into* Ireland?" cried the young wife suddenly.

"Yes—you've been riding backwards: if we were going the other way, 'twould be a different story." And the lady in the raincoat looked at her wisely.

The train was grinding to a stop at a large station in Wales. The schoolgirl, after one paralyzed moment, rose and got off through the corridor in a dream; the book she closed was seen to be *Black Stallion of the Downs*. A big tall man climbed on and took her place. It was this station, it was felt, where they actually ceased leaving a place and from now on were arriving at one.

The tall Welshman drove into the compartment through any remarks that were going on and with great strength like a curse heaved his bag on top of several of theirs in the rack, where it had been thought there was no more room, and took the one seat without question. With serious sets of his shoulders he settled down in the middle of them, between Victor and the lady in the raincoat, facing the man from Connemara. His hair was in two corner bushes, and he had a full eye—like that of the horse in the storm in old chromos in the West of America—the kind of eye supposed to attract lightning. In the silence of the dreary stop, he slapped all his pockets—not having forgotten anything, only making sure. His hands were powdered over with something fairly black.

"Well! How far do *you* go?" he put to the man from Connemara and then to them in turn, and each time the answer came, "Ireland." He seemed unduly astonished.

He lighted a pipe, and pointed it toward the little boy. "What have you been doing in England, eh?"

Victor writhed forward and set his teeth into the strap of the outer door.

"He's been to a wedding," said the young wife, as though she and Victor were saying the same thing in two different ways, and smiled on him fully for the first time.

"Who got married?"

"Me brother," Victor said in a strangled voice, still holding on recklessly while the train, starting with a jerk, rocked him to the side.

"Big wedding?"

Two greyhounds in plaid blankets, like dangerously ecstatic old ladies hoping no one would see them, rushed into, out of, then past the corridor door which the incoming Welshman had failed to shut behind him. The glare in the eye of the man who followed, with his belt flying about him as he pulled back on the dogs, was wild, too.

"Big wedding?"

"Me family was all over the place if that's what you mean." Victor wildly chewed; there was a smell of leather.

"Ah, it has driven his poor mother to her bed, it was that grand a wedding," said the young wife. "That's why she's in England, and Victor here on his own."

"You must have missed school. What school do you go to—you *go* to school?" By the power of his eye, the Welshman got Victor to let go the strap and answer yes or no.

"School, yes."

"You study French and so on?"

"Ah, them languages is no good. What good is Irish?" said Victor passionately, and somebody said, "Now what does your mother tell you?"

"What ails your mother?" said the Welshman.

"Ah, it's her old trouble. Ask *her*. But there's two of me brothers at one end and five at the other."

"You're divided."

The young wife let Victor stand on the seat and haul her paper parcel off the rack so she could give him an orange. She drew out as well a piece of needlepoint, square and tarnished, which she spread over her pretty arm and hung before their eyes.

"Beautiful!"

" 'A Wee Cottage' is the name it has."

"I see the cottage. 'Tis very wee, and so's every bit about it."

" 'Twould blind you: 'tis a work of art."

"The little rabbit peeping out!"

"Makes you wish you had your gun," said the Welshman to Victor.

The young wife said, "Me grandmother. At eighty she died, very sudden, on a visit to England. God rest her soul. Now I'm bringing this masterpiece home to Ireland."

"Who could blame you."

"Well you should bring it away, all those little stitches she put in."

She wrapped it away, just as anyone could see her—as she might for the moment see herself—folding a blanket down into the crib and tucking the ends. Victor, now stained and fragrant with orange, leapt like a tiger to pop the parcel back overhead.

"No, I shouldn't think learning Irish would do you much good," said the Welshman. "No real language."

"Why not?" said the lady in the raincoat instantly. "I've a brother who is a very fluent Irish speaker and a popular man. You cannot doubt yourself that when the English hear you speaking a tongue they cannot follow,

in the course of time they are due to start holding respect
for you."

"From London you are." The Welshman bit down on
his pipe and smoked.

"*Oh* my God." The man from Connemara struck his
head. "I have an English wife. How would she like that,
I wouldn't like to know? If all at once I begun on her in
Irish! How would you like it if your husband would only
speak to you in Irish? Or Welsh, my God?" He searched
the eyes of all the women, and last of the young Irish
sweetheart—who did not seem to grasp the question. "Aha
ha ha!" he cried urgently and despairingly at her, asking
her only to laugh with him.

But the young man's arm was thrust along the seat and
she was sitting under its arch as if it were the entrance
to a cave, which surely they all must see.

"Will you eat a biscuit now?" the young wife gently
asked the man from Connemara. He took one wordlessly;
for the moment he had no English or Irish. So she broke
open another paper parcel beside her. "I have oceans,"
she said.

"Oh, *you wait*," said the lady in the raincoat, rising.
And *she* opened a parcel as big as a barrel and it was full
of everything to eat that anybody could come out of England with alive.

She offered candy, jam roll, biscuits, bananas, nuts, sec-
tions of bursting orange, and bread and butter, and they
all in the flush of the hospitality and heat sat eating.
Everybody partook but the Welshman, who had presumably had a dinner in Wales. It was more than ever like
a little party, all the finer somehow, sadly enough, for the
nose against the windowpane. They poured out tea from
a couple of steaming thermoses; the black windows—for

the sun was down now, never having been out of the fogs and rains all day—coated warmly over between them and what flew by out there.

"Could you tell me the name of a place to stay in Cork?" The American girl spoke up to the man from Connemara as he gave her a biscuit.

"In Cork? Ah, but you don't want to be stopping in Cork. Killarney is where you would do well to go, if you're wanting to see the wonders of Ireland. The lakes and the hills! Blue as blue skies, the lakes. That's where you want to go, Killarney."

"She wants to climb the Hill of Tara, you mean," said the guard, who with a burst of cold wind had entered to punch their tickets again. "All the way up, and into the raths, too, to lay her eyes by the light of candles on something she's never seen before; if that's what she's after. Have you never climbed the Hill and never crept into those, lady? Maybe 'twould take a little boost from behind, I don't know your size; but I think 'twould not be difficult getting you through." He gave her ticket its punch, with a keen blue glance at her, and banged out.

"Well, *I'm* going to the sitting in the dining car now." The lady in the raincoat stood up under the dim little lights in the ceiling that shone on her shoulders. Then down her long nose she suggested to them each to come, too. Did she really mean to eat still, and after all that largess? They laughed, as if to urge her by their shock to go on, and the American girl witlessly murmured, "No, I have a letter to write."

Off she went, that long coat shimmering and rattling. The little boy looked after her, the first sea wind blew in at the opened door, and his cowlick nodded like a dark flower.

"Very grand," said the Connemara man. "Very high and mighty she is, indeed."

Out there, nuns, swept by untoward blasts of wind, shrieked soundlessly as in nightmares in the corridors. It must be like the Tunnel of Love for them—the thought drifted into the young sweetheart's head.

She was so stiff! She struggled up, staggered a little as she left the compartment. All alone she stood in the corridor. A young man went past, soft fair mustache, soft fair hair, combing the hair—oh, delicious. Here came a hat like old Cromwell's on a lady, who had also a fur cape, a stick, flat turning-out shoes, and a heavy book with a pencil in it. The old lady beat her stick on the floor and made a sweet old man in gaiters and ribbon-tied hat back up into a doorway to let her by. All these people were going into the dining cars. She hung her head out the open corridor window into the Welsh night, which, seen from inside itself—her head in its mouth—could look not black but pale. Wales was formidable, barrier-like. What contours which she could not see were raised out there, dense and heraldic? Once there was a gleam from their lights on the walls of a tunnel, from the everlasting springs that the tunnelers had cut. Should they ever have started, those tunnelers? Sometimes there were sparks. She hung out into the wounded night a minute: let him wish her back.

"What do you do with yourself in England, keep busy?" said the man from Wales, pointing the stem of his pipe at the man from Connemara.

"I do, I raise birds in Sussex, if you're asking my hobby."

"A terrific din, I daresay. Birds keep you awake all night?"

"On the contrary. Never notice it for a minute. Of course there are the birds that engage in conversation rather than sing. I might be listening to the conversation."

"Parrots, you mean. You have parrots? You teach them to talk?"

"Budgies, man. Oh, I did have one that was a lovely talker, but curious, very strange and curious, in his habits of feeding."

"What was it he ate? How much would you ask for a bird like that?"

"Like what?"

"Parrot that could talk but didn't eat well, that you were just mentioning you had."

"That bird was an exception. Not for sale."

"Are you responsible for your birds?"

They all sat waiting while a tunnel banged.

"What do you mean responsible?"

"Responsible: you sell me a bird. Presently he doesn't talk or sing. Can I bring it back?"

"You cannot. That's God-given, lads."

"How old is the bird now? Good health?"

"Owing to conditions in England I could not get him the specialties he liked, and came in one morning to find the bird stiff. Still it's a nice hobby. Very interesting."

"Would you have got five pounds for this bird if you had found a customer for her? What was it the bird craved so?"

" 'Twas a male, not on the market, and if there had been another man, that would sell him to you, 'twould have cost you eight pounds."

"Ah. He ate inappropriate food?"

"You might say he *could not get* inappropriate food. He was destroyed by a mortal appetite for food you'd call it unlikely for a bird to desire at all. Myself, I never raised a bird that thrived so, learned faster, and had more to say."

"You never tried to sell him."

"For one thing I could not afford to turn him loose in Sussex. I told my wife not to be dusting his cage without due caution, not to be talking to him so much herself, the way she did."

The Welshman looked at him. He said, "Well, he died."

"Pass by my house!" cried the man from Connemara. "And look in the window, as you'll likely do, and you'll see the bird—stuffed. You'll think he's alive at first. Open beak! Talking up to the last, like you or I that have souls to be saved."

"Souls: Is the leading church in Ireland Catholic, would you call Ireland a Catholic country?" The Welshman settled himself anew.

"I would, yes."

"Is there a Catholic church where you live, in your town?"

"There is."

"And you go?"

"I do."

"Suppose you miss. If you miss going to church, does the priest fine you for it?"

"Of course he does not! Father Lavery! What do you mean?"

"Suppose it's Sunday—tomorrow's Sunday—and you don't go to church. Would you have to pay a fine to the priest?"

The man from Connemara lowered his dark head; he glared at the lovers—for she had returned to her place. "Of course I would not!" Still he looked at the girl.

"Ah, in the windows black as they are, we do look almost like ghosts riding by," she breathed, looking past him.

He said at once, "A castle I know, you see them on the wall."

"What castle?" said the sweetheart.

"You mean what ghosts. First she comes, then he comes."

"In Connemara?"

"Ah, you've never been there. Late tomorrow night I'll be there. She comes first because she's mad, and he slow —got the dagger stuck in him, you see? Destroyed by her. She walks along, carries herself grand, not shy. Then he comes, unwilling, not touching with his feet—pulled through the air. By the dagger, you might say, like a hooked fish. Because they're a pair, himself and herself, sure as they was joined together—and while you look go leaping in the bright air, moonlight as may be, and sailing off together cozy as a couple of kites to start it again."

That girl's straight hair, cut like a little train to a point at the nape of her neck, her little pointed nose that came down in the one unindented line which began at her hair, her swimming, imagining eyes, held them all, like her lover, perfectly still. Love was amazement now. The lovers did not touch, for a thousand reasons, but that was one.

"Start what again?" said the Welshman. "Have you personally seen them?"

"I have, I'm no exception."

"Can you say who they might be?"

"Visit the neighborhood for yourself and there'll be those who can acquaint you with the gory details. Myself I'm acquainted with only the general idea of their character and disposition, formed after putting two and two together. Have you never seen a ghost, then?"

The Welshman gave a look as if he'd been unfairly

struck, as if a question coming at him now in here was carrying things too far. But he only said, "Heard them."

"Ah, do keep it to yourself then, for the duration of the journey, and not go bragging, will you?" the young wife cried at him. "Irish ghosts are enough for some of us for the one night without mixing them up with the Welsh and them shrieking things, and just before all of us are going on the water except yourself."

"You don't mind the Lord and Lady Beagle now, do you? They shouldn't frighten you, they're lovely and married. Married still. Why, their names just come to me, did you hear that? Lord and Lady Beagle—like they sent in a card. Ha! Ha!" Again the man from Connemara tried to bring that singing laugh out of the frightened sweetheart, from whom he had not yet taken his glances away.

"Don't," the young wife begged him, forcing her eyes to his salver-like palm. "Those are wild, crazy names for ghosts."

"Well, what kind of ghosts do you think they ever are!" Their glances met through their laughter and remorse. She tossed her head.

"There ain't no ghosts," said Victor.

"Now suck this good orange," she whispered to him, as if he were being jealous.

"Here comes the bride," announced the Welshman.

"*Oh* my God." But what business was she of the Welshman's?

In came the lady in the raincoat beaming from her dinner, but he talked right around her hip. "Do you have to confess?" he said. "Regularly? Suppose you make a confession—swear words, lewd thoughts, or the like: *then* does the priest make you pay a fine?"

"Confession's free, why not?" remarked the lady, stepping over all their feet.

"You're a Catholic, too?" he said, as she hung above his knee.

And as they all closed their eyes she fell into his lap, right down on top of him. Even the dogs, now rushing along in the other direction, hung on the air a moment, their tongues out. Then one dog was inside with them. This greyhound flung herself forward, back, down to the floor, her tail slapped out like a dragon's. Her eyes gazed toward the confusion, and little bubbles of boredom and suspicion played under the skin of her jowls, puff, puff, puff, while wrinkles of various memories and agitations came and went on her forehead like little forks of lightning.

"Well, look what's with us," said the lover. "Here, lad, here, lad."

"That's Telephone Girl," said the lady in the raincoat, now on her feet and straightening herself with distant sweepings of both hands. "I was just in conversation with the keeper of those. Don't be getting her stirred up. She's a winner, he has it." She let herself down into the seat and spread a look on all of them as if she had always been too womanly for the place. Her mooning face turned slowly and met the Welshman's stern, strong glance: *he* appeared to be expecting some apology from some source.

" 'Tisn't everybody runs so fast and gets nothing for it in the end herself, either," said the lady. Telephone Girl shuddered, ate some crumbs, coughed.

"I'm ashamed to hear you saying that, she gets the glory," said the man from Connemara. "How many human beings of your acquaintance get half a dog's chance at glory?"

"You don't like dogs." The lady looked at him, bowing her head.

"They're not my element. That's not the way I'm made, no."

The man in charge rushed in, and out he and the dog shot together. Somebody closed the door; it was the Welshman.

"Now: what time of the night do you get to Cork?" he asked.

The lover spoke, unexpectedly. "Tomorrow morning." The girl let out a long breath after him.

"What time of the morning?"

"Nine!" shouted everybody but the American.

"Travel all night," he said.

"Book a berth in Fishguard!"

The mincing woman with the red-haired baby boy passed —the baby with his same fat, enchanted squint looked through the glass at them.

"Oh, I always get seasick!" cried the young wife in fatalistic enthusiastic tones, only distantly watching the baby, who, although he stretched his little hand against the glass, was not being kidnaped now. She leaned over to tell the young girl, "Let me only step off the train at Fishguard and I'm dying already."

"What do you usually do for an attack of seasickness when you're on the Cork boat?"

"*I* just stay in one place and never move, that's what *I* do!" she cried, the smile that had never left her sad, sweet lips turned upon them all. "I don't try to move at all and I die all the way." Victor edged a little away from her.

"The boat rocks," suggested the Welshman. Victor edged away from him.

"The *Innisfallen?* Of course she rocks, there's a far,

wide sea, very deep and treacherous, and very historic."
The man from Connemara folded his arms.

"It takes six weeks, don't you think?" The young wife
appealed to them all. "To get over the journey. I tell me
husband, a fortnight is never enough. Me husband is English, though. I've never liked England. I have six aunts
all living there, too. Me mother's sisters." She smiled.
"They all are hating it. Me grandmother died while she
was in England."

His cheeks sunk on his fists, Victor leaned forward over
his knees. His hair, blue-black, whorled around the cowlick like a spinning gramophone record; he seemed to
dream of being down on the ground, and fighting somebody on it.

"God rest her soul," said the lady in the raincoat, as
if she might have passed through the goods car and seen
where Grandmother was riding with them, to her grave in
Ireland; but in that case the young wife would have been
with the dead, and not playing at mother with Victor.

"Then how much does the passage cost you? Fishguard
to Cork, Cork back to Fishguard? I may decide to try it
on holiday sometime."

"Where are you leaving us this night?" asked the young
wife, still in the voice in which she had spoken of her
grandmother and her mother's sisters.

He gave out a name to make her look more commiser-
ating, and repeated, "What is the fare from Fishguard
to Cork?"

They stopped just then at a dark station and a paper
boy's voice called his papers into the train.

"*Oh* my God. Where are we!"

The Welshman put up his finger and called for a paper,
and one was brought inside to him by a strange, dark
child.

At the sight of the man opening his newspaper, the lady in the raincoat spoke promptly and with her lips wooden, like an actress. "How did the race come out?"

"What's that? Race? What race would that be?" He gave her that look he gave her the time she sat down on him. He stretched and rattled his paper without exposing it too widely to anybody.

She tilted her head. "Little Boy Blue, yes," she murmured over his shoulder.

A discussion of Little Boy Blue arose while he kept on reading.

"How much money at a time do you bet on the races?" the Welshman asked suddenly, coming out from behind the paper. Then as suddenly he retreated, taking back the question entirely.

"Now the second race," murmured the lady in the raincoat. Everybody wreathed in the Welshman. He was in the middle of the Welsh news, silent as the dead.

The man from Connemara put up a hand as the page might have been turned, "Long Gone the favorite! You were long gone yourself," he added politely to the lady in the raincoat. Possibly she had been punished enough for going out to eat and coming in to fall down all over a man.

"Yes I was," she said, lifting her chin; she brought out a Player and lighted it herself. She puffed. " 'Twas a long way, twelve cars. 'Twas a lovely dinner—chicken. One man rose up in the aisle when it was put before him and gave a cry, 'It's rabbit!' "

They were pleased. The man from Connemara gave his high, free laugh. The lovers were strung like bows in silent laughter, but the lady blew a ring of smoke, at which Victor aimed an imaginary weapon.

"A lovely, long dinner. A man left us but returned to

the car to say that while we were eating they shifted the
carriages about and he had gone up the train, down the
train, and could not find himself at all." Her voice was
so moody and remote now it might be some wandering of
long ago she spoke to them about.

The Welshman said, over his paper, "Shifted the carriages?"

All laughed the harder.

"He said his carriage was gone, yes. From where he
had left it: he hoped to find it yet, but I don't think he
has. He came back the second time to the dining car and
spoke about it. He laid his hand on the guard's arm.
'While I was sitting at the table and eating my dinner,
the carriages have been shifted about,' he said. 'I wandered through the cars with the dogs running and cars
with boxes in them, and through cars with human beings
sitting in them I never laid eyes on in the journey—one
party going on among some young people that would altogether block the traffic in the corridor.' "

"All Irish," said the young wife, and smoothed Victor's
head; he looked big-eyed into space.

"The guard was busy and spoke to a third party, a
gentleman eating. Yes, they were, all Irish. 'Will you mer-
cifully take and show this gentleman where he is traveling, when you can, since he's lost?' 'Not lost,' he said,
'distracted,' and went through his system of argument.
The gentleman said he could jolly well find his own carriage. The man opposite him rose up and that was when
he declared the chicken was rabbit. The gentleman put
down his knife and said man lost or not, carriage shifted
or not, the stew rabbit or not, the man could just the
same fight back to where he had come from, as he himself jolly well intended to do when he could finish the

dinner on his plate in peace." She opened her purse, and passed licorice drops around.

"He sounds vulgar," said the man from Connemara.

" 'Twas a lovely dinner."

"*You* weren't lost, I take it?" said the Welshman, accepting a licorice drop. "Traveled much?"

"Oh dear Heaven, traveled? Well, I have. Yes, no end to it."

"*Oh* my God."

"No, *I'm* never lost."

"Let's drop the subject," said the Welshman.

The lovers settled back into the cushions. They were the one subject nobody was going to discuss.

"Look," the young girl said in a low voice, from within the square of the young man's arm, but not to him. "I see a face that keeps going past, looking through the window. A man, plying up and down, could he be the one so unfortunate?"

"Not him, he's leading greyhounds, didn't we see him come in?" The young man spoke eagerly, to them all. "Leading, or they leading him."

" 'Tis a long train," the lady murmured to the Welshman. "The longest, most populated train leaving England, I would suppose, the one going over to catch the *Innisfallen*."

"Is that the name of the boat? You were glad to leave England?"

"It is and I was—pleased to be starting my journey, pleased to have it over." She gave a look at him—then at the others, the compartment, the tumbled baggage, everything. Outside, dim Wales clapped strongly at the window, like some accompanying bird. "I'll just lower the shade, will I?" she said.

She pulled at the window shade and fastened it down,

and pulled down the door shade after it. The minute she did that, the window shade flew up, with a noise like a turkey.

They shouted for joy—they knew it! She *was* funny.

The train stopped and waited a long time in the dark, out from nowhere. They sat awhile, swung their feet; the man from Connemara whistled for a minute marvelously, Victor had his third orange.

"Suppose we're late!" shouted the man from Connemara. The mountains could hear him; they had opened the window to look out hoping to see the trouble, but could not. "And the *Innisfallen* sails without us! And we don't reach the other side in this night!"

"Then you'll all have to spend the night in Fishguard," said the Welshman.

"Oh, what a scene there'll be in Cork, when we don't arrive!" cried the young wife merrily. "When the boat sails in without us, oh poor souls."

Victor laughed harshly. He had made a pattern with his orange peel on the window ledge, which he now swept away.

"There's none too much room for the traveler in the town of Fishguard," said the Welshman over his pipe. "You'll do best to keep dry in the station."

"Won't they *die* of it in Cork?" The young wife cocked her head.

"Me five brothers will stand ready to give me a beating!" Victor said, then looked proud.

"I daresay it won't be the first occasion you've put in the night homeless in Fishguard."

"In Fishguard?" warningly cried the man from Connemara. A scowl lit up his face and his eyes opened wide with innocence. "Didn't you know this was the boat train you're riding, man?"

"Oh, is that what you call it?" said the Welshman in equal innocence.

"They *hold* the boat for us. I feel it's safe to say that every soul on board this train saving yourself is riding to catch the boat."

"Hold the *Innisfallen* at Fishguard Harbor? For how long?"

"If need be till doomsday, but we are generally sailing at midnight."

"No sir, we'll never be left helpless in Fishguard, this or any other night," said the lady in the raincoat.

"Or!" cried the man from Connemara. "Or! We could take the other boat if we're as late as that, to Rosslare, oh my God! And spend the Sunday bringing ourselves back to Cork!"

"You're going to Connemara to see your mother," the young wife said psychically.

"I'm sure as God's truth staying the one night in Cork first!" he shouted across at her, and banged himself on the knees, as if they were trying to take Cork away from him.

The Welshman asked, "What is the longest on record they have ever held the boat?"

"Who knows?" said the lady in the raincoat. "Maybe 'twill be tonight."

"Only can I get out now and see where we've stopped?" asked Victor.

"*Oh* my God—we've started! *Oh* that Cork City!"

"When you travel to Cork, do the lot of you generally get seasick?" inquired the Welshman, swaying among them as they got under way.

The lady in the raincoat made him a grand gesture

with one hand, and rose and pulled down her suitcase. She opened it and fetched out from beneath the hot water bottle in pink flannel a little pasteboard box.

"What's that going to be—pills for seasickness?" he said.

She lifted the lid and passed the box under his eyes and then under their eyes, although too fast to be quite offering anything. " 'Tis a present," she said. "A present of seasick pills, given me for the journey."

The lovers smiled simultaneously, as they would at the thought of any present.

The train stopped again, started; stopped, started. Here on the outer edge of Wales it advanced and hesitated as rhythmically and as interminably as a needle in a hem. The wheels had taken on that defenseless sound peculiar to running near the open sea. Oil lamps burned in their little boxes at the halts; there was a pull at the heart from the feeling of the trees all being bent the same way.

"*Now* where?" They had stopped again.

A sigh escaped the lovers, who had drawn a breath of the sea. A single lamp stared in at their window, like the eye of a dragon lifted out of the lid of sleep.

"It's my station!" The Welshman suddenly addressed himself. He reared up, banged down the bushes on his head under a black hat, collected his suitcase and overcoat, and almost swept away with it the parcel with the "Wee Cottage" in it, belonging to the young wife. He got past them, dragging his suitcase with a great heave of the shoulder—God knew what was inside. He wrenched open the door, turned and looked at the lot of them, and then gently backed down into the outdoors.

Only to reappear. He had mistaken the station after all.

But he simply held his ground there in the doorway, brazening it out as the train darted on.

"I may decide on raising my own birds some day," he said in a somewhat louder voice. "What did you begin with, a cock and a hen?"

On the index finger which the man from Connemara raised before he answered was a black fingernail, like the mark of a hammer blow; it might have been a reminder not to do something or other before he got home to Ireland.

"I would advise you to begin with a cock and two hens. Don't go into it without getting advice."

"What did you start with?"

"Six cocks—"

Another dark station, and down the Welshman dropped.

"And six hens!"

It was almost too much that his face rose there *again*. He wasn't embarrassed at himself, any more than he was by how black and all impenetrable it was outside in Wales, and asked, "Do you have to produce a passport to go into Ireland?"

"Certainly, a passport or a travel card. *Oh* my God."

"What do you mean by a travel card? Let me see yours. Every one of you carry one with you?"

Travel cards and passports were produced and handed up to him.

"Oh, how beautiful your mother is!" cried the young wife to Victor, over his shoulder. "Is that a wee strawberry mark she has there on her cheek?"

" 'Tis!" he cried in agony.

The Welshman was holding the American's different-looking passport open in his hand; she looked startled, herself, that she had given it up and at once, as if this were required and he had waked her up in the night. He read out her name, nationality, age, her husband's name, nationality. It was not that he read it officially—worse: as if it were a poem in the paper, only with the last verse missing.

"My husband is a photographer. We've made a little darkroom in our flat," she told him.

But he all at once turned back and asked the man from Connemara, "And you give it as your opinion your prize bird died of longings for food from far away."

"There've been times when I've dreamed a certain *person* may have had more to do with it!" the man from Connemara cried in crescendo. "That I've never mentioned till now. But women are jealous and uncertain creatures, I've been thinking as we came this long way along tonight."

"Of *birds!*" cried the young wife, her fingers going to her shoulders.

"Name your poison."

"Why birds?"

"Why not?"

"Because it talked?"

"Name your poison."

Another lantern, another halt of the train.

"It'll be raining over the water," the Welshman called as he swung open his door. From the step he looked back and said, "What do you take the seasick pills in, have you drink to take them in?"

"I have."

He said out of the windy night, "Can you buy drink on board the ship? Or is it not too late for that?"

"Three miles out 'tis only the sea and glory," shouted the man from Connemara.

"Be good," the Welshman tossed back at him, and quite

lightly he dropped away. He disappeared for the third time into the Welsh black, this time for keeps. It was as though a big thumb had snuffed him out.

They smoothed and straightened themselves behind him, all but the young lovers spreading out in the seats; she rubbed her arm, up and down. Not a soul had inquired of that poor vanquished man what he did, if he had wife and children living—he might have only had an auntie. They never let him tell what he was doing with himself in either end of Wales, or why he had to come on this very night, or even what in the world he was carrying in that heavy case.

As they talked, the American girl laid her head back, a faint smile on her face.

"Just one word of advice," said the man from Connemara in her ear, putting her passport, warm from his hand, into hers. "Be careful in future who you ask questions of. You were safe when you spoke to me, I'm a married man. I was pleased to tell you what I could—go to Killarney and so forth and so on, see the marvelous beauty of the lakes. But next time ask a guard."

Victor's head tumbled against the watchful side of the young wife, his right hand was flung in her lap, a fist floating away. In Fishguard, they had to shake him awake and pull him out into the rain.

No traveler out of that compartment was, actually, booked for a berth on the *Innisfallen* except the lady in the raincoat, who marched straight off. Most third-class train passengers spent the night third-class in the *Innisfallen* lounge. The man from Connemara was the first one stretched, a starfish of exhaustion, on a cretonne-covered couch. The American girl stared at a page of her book, then closed it until they were under way. The lovers disappeared. In the deeps of night that bright room reached some vortex of quiet, like a room where all brains are at work and great decisions are on the brink. Occasionally there was a tapping, as of drumming fingernails—that meant to closed or hypnotized eyes that dogs were being sped through. The random, gentle old men who were walking the corridors in their tweeds and seemed lost as Jesus's lambs, were waiting perhaps for the bar to open. The young wife, as desperate as she'd feared, saw nothing, forgot everything, and even abandoned Victor, as if there could never be any time or place in the world but this of her suffering. She spoke to the child as if she had never seen him before and would never see him again. Victor took the last little paper of biscuits she had given him away to a corner and slowly emptied it, making a mountain of the crumbs; then he bent his head over his travel card with its new stamp, on which presently he rolled his cheek and floated unconscious.

Once the man from Connemara sat up out of his sleep and stared at the American girl pinned to her chair across the room, as if he saw somebody desperate who had left her husband once, endangered herself among strangers, been turned back, and was here for the second go-round, asking again for a place to stay in Cork. She stared back motionless, until he was a starfish again.

Then it was morning—a world of sky coursing above, streaming light. The *Innisfallen* had entered the Lee. Almost at arm's reach were the buff, pink, gray, salmon fronts of houses, trees shining like bird wings, and bells that jumped toward sound as the ship, all silent, flowed past. The Sunday, the hour, too, were encroaching-real. Each lawn had a flag-like purity that braved and invited all the morning senses, even smell, as snow can—as if snow had fallen in the night, and this sun and this ship had come to trace it and melt it.

It was that passing, short, yet inviolate distance between ship and land on both sides that made an arrow-like question in the heart. Someone cried at random, "What town is this?" Any of them should have known, but the senses waked back home can fill too full, until black lines and framework vanish like names, leaving only shapes of light and color without knowledge or memory to inform them.

To wake up to the river, no longer the sea! There was more than one little town, that in their silent going they saluted while not touching or deviating to it at all. After the length of the ship had passed a ringing steeple, and the hands had glinted gold at them from the clockface, an older, harsher, more distant bell rang from an inland time: *now*.

Now sea gulls paced city lawns. *They* moved through the hedges, the ship in the garden. A thrush could be heard singing, and there he sang—so clear and so early it all was. On deck a little girl clapped her hands. "Why do you do that!" her brother lovingly encouraged her.

On shore a city street appeared, and now cars were following the ship along; passengers inside blew auto horns and waved handkerchiefs up and down. There was a sidewise sound of a harmonica, frantic, tiny and bold. Victor was up where he ought not to be on deck, handing out black frowns and tunes to the docks sliding into sight. Now he had to look out for his brothers. Perhaps deep in the lounge his guardian was now sleeping at last, white and exhausted, inhumanly smiling in her sleep.

The lovers stood on the lower, more shaded deck—two backs. A line of sun was between them like a thread that could be picked off. One ought not yet to look into their

faces, watching water. How far, how deep was this day
to cut into their hearts? From now on everything would
cut deeper than yesterday. Her wintry boots stiff from
their London wet looked big on the ship, pricked with
ears, at that brink of light they hung over. And suddenly
she changed position—one shoe tapped, pointing, back of
the other. She poised there. The boat whistle thundered
like a hundred organ notes, but she did not quake—now
as used to boat whistles as one of the sea gulls; or as far
away.

"There's a bride on board!" called somebody. "Look at
her, look!"

Sure enough, a girl who had not yet showed herself
in public now appeared by the rail in a white spring hat
and, over her hands, a little old-fashioned white bunny
muff. She stood there all ready to be met, now come out
in her own sweet time. Delight gathered all around, singing began on board, bells could by now be heard ringing
urgently in the town. Surely that color beating in their
eyes came from flags hung out up the looming shore.
The bride smiled but did not look up; she was looking
down at her dazzling little fur muff.

They were in, the water held still about them. The gulls
converged; just under the surface a newspaper slowly
went down with its drowned news.

In the crowd of the dock, the lady in the raincoat was
being confronted with a flock of beautiful children—red
flags in their cheeks, caps on their heads, little black
boots like pipes—and by a man bigger than she was. He
stood smoking while the children hurled themselves up
against her. As people hurried around her carrying their
bundles and bags in the windy bright of the Cork dock,
she stood camouflaged like a sportsman in his own poly-

chrome fields, a hand on her striped hip. Vague, luminous, smiling, her big white face held a moment and bent down for its kiss. The man from Connemara strode by, looking down on her as if now her head were in the basket. His cap set at a fairly desperate angle, he went leaping into the streets of Cork City.

Victor was shouting at the top of his lungs, "Here I am!" The young wife, coming forth old but still alive, was met by old women in cloaks, three young men to embrace her, and a donkey and cart to ride her home, once she had put Victor with his brothers.

Perhaps regardless of the joy or release of an arrival, or because of it, there is always for someone a last-minute, finger-like touch, a reminder, a promise of confusion. Behind shut lids the American girl saw the customs' chalk mark just now scrawled on the wall of her suitcase. Like a gypsy's sign found on her own front door, it stared at her from the sensitized optic dark, and she felt exposed—as if, in spite of herself, when she didn't know it, something had been told on her. "A rabbit ran over my grave," she thought. She left her suitcase in the parcel room and walked out into Cork.

When it rained late in that afternoon, the American girl was still in Cork, and stood sheltering in the doorway of a pub. She was listening to the pub sounds and the alley sounds as she might to a garden's and a fountain's.

She had had her day, her walk, that began at the red, ferny, echo-hung rock against which the lowest houses were set, where the ocean-river sent up signals of mirrored light. She had walked the hill and crossed the swan-bright bridges, her way wound in among people busy at encounters, meetings, it seemed to her reunions. After church in the streets of Cork dozens of little girls in confirmation dresses, squared off by their veils into animated paper snowflakes, raced and danced out of control and into charmed traffic—like miniature and more conscious brides. The trees had almost rushed with light and blossom; they nearly had sound, as the bells did. Boughs that rocked on the hill were tipped and weighted as if with birds, which were really their own bursting and almost-bursting leaves. In all Cork today every willow stood with gold-red hair springing and falling about it, like Venus alive. Rhododendrons swam in light, leaves and flowers alike; only a shadow could separate them into colors. She had felt no lonelier than that little bride herself, who had come off the boat. Yes, somewhere in the crowd at the dock there must have been a young man holding flowers: he had been taken for granted.

In the future would the light, that had jumped like the man from Connemara into the world, be a memory, like that of a meeting, or must there be mere faith that it had been like that?

Shielding the telegraph-form from her fellow writers at the post-office table, she printed out to her husband in England, "England was a mistake." At once she scratched that out, and took back the blame but without words.

Love with the joy being drawn out of it like anything else that aches—that was loneliness; not this. *I* was nearly destroyed, she thought, and again was threatened with a light head, a rush of laughter, as when the Welshman had come so far with them and then let them off.

If she could never tell her husband her secret, perhaps she would never tell it at all. You must never betray pure joy—the kind you were born and began with—either by hiding it or by parading it in front of people's eyes; they didn't want to be shown it. And still you must tell it. Is there no way? she thought—for here I am, this far. I see Cork's streets take off from the waterside and rise lifting their houses and towers like note above note on a page of music, with arpeggios running over it of green and galleries and belvederes, and the bright sun raining at the top. Out of the joy I hide for fear it is promiscuous, I may walk for ever at the fall of evening by the river, and find this river street by the red rock, this first, last house, that's perhaps a boarding house now, standing full-face to the tide, and look up to that window—that upper window, from which the mystery will never go. The curtains dyed so many times over are still pulled back and the window looks out open to the evening, the river, the hills, and the sea.

For a moment someone—she thought it was a woman—came and stood at the window, then hurled a cigarette with its live coal down into the extinguishing garden. But it was not the impatient tenant, it was the window itself that could tell her all she had come here to know—or all she could bear this evening to know, and that was light and rain, light and rain, dark, light, and rain.

"Don't expect me back yet" was all she need say tonight in the telegram. What was always her trouble? "You hope for too much," he said.

When early this morning the bride smiled, it might almost have been for her photograph; but she still did not look up—as though if even her picture were taken, she would vanish. And now she had vanished.

Walking on through the rainy dusk, the girl again took shelter in the warm doorway of the pub, holding her message, unfinished and unsent.

"Ah, it's a heresy, I told him," a man inside was shouting, out of the middle of his story. A barmaid glimmered through the passage in her frill, a glad cry went up at her entrance, as if she were the heresy herself, and when they all called out something fresh it was like the signal for a song.

The girl let her message go into the stream of the street, and opening the door walked into the lovely room full of strangers.

Ladies in Spring

The pair moved through that gray landscape as though no one would see them—dressed alike in overalls and faded coats, one big, one little, one black-headed, one tow-headed, father and son. Each carried a cane fishing pole over his shoulder, and Dewey carried the bucket in his other hand. It was a soft, gray, changeable day overhead—the first like that, here in the month of March.

Just a quarter of an hour before, Dewey riding to school in the school bus had spotted his father walking right down the road, the poles on his shoulder—two poles. Dewey skimmed around the schoolhouse door, and when his father came walking through Royals, he was waiting at the tree by the post office.

"Scoot. Get on back in the schoolhouse. You been told," said his father.

In a way, Dewey would have liked to obey that: Miss Pruitt had promised to read them about *Excalibur*. What had made her go and pick today?

"But I can see you're bound to come," said his father. "Only we ain't going to catch us no fish, because there ain't no water left to catch 'em in."

"The river!"

"All but dry."

"You been many times already?"

84

"Son, this is my first time this year. Might as well keep still about it at home."

The sky moved, soft and wet and gray, but the ground underfoot was powder dry. Where an old sycamore had blown over the spring before, there was turned up a tough round wall of roots and clay all white, like the moon on the ground. The river had not backed up into the old backing places. Vines, leafless and yet abundant and soft, covered the trees and thickets as if rainclouds had been dropped down from the sky over them. The swamp looked gray and endless as pictures in the Bible; wherever Dewey turned, the world held perfectly still for moments at a time—then a heron would pump through.

"Papa, what's that lady doing?"

"Why, I believe that's Miss Hattie Purcell on foot ahead."

"Is she supposed to be way out here?"

"Miss Hattie calls herself a rainmaker, son. She could be at it. We sure can use the rain. She's most generally on hand at the post office."

"I know now." He opened his mouth.

"Don't be so apt to holler," said his father. "We may can keep to the rear of her, if we try good."

The back of Miss Hattie rose up a little steep place, her black hat sharp above the trees. She was ahead of them by a distance no longer than the street of Royals. Her black coat was a roomy winter one and hung down in the back to her ankles, when it didn't catch on things. She was carrying, like a rolling pin, a long furled umbrella, and moved straight forward in some kind of personal zigzag of a walk—it would be hard to pass *her*.

Now Miss Hattie dipped out of sight into a gully.

"Miss Hattie's making a beeline, ain't she," said Dewey's father. "Look at her go. Let's you and me take us a plain *path*."

But as they came near the river in a little while, Dewey pointed his finger. Fairly close, through the trees, they saw a big strong purse with a handle on it like a suitcase, set down on the winter leaves. Another quiet step and they could see Miss Hattie. There on the ground, with her knees drawn up the least bit, skirt to her ankles, coat spread around her like a rug, hat over her brow, steel glasses in her hand, sat Miss Hattie Purcell, bringing rain. She did not even see them.

Miss Hattie brought rain by sitting a vigil of the necessary duration beside the nearest body of water, as everybody knew. She made no more sound at it than a man fishing. But something about the way Miss Hattie's comfort shoes showed their tips below her skirt and carried a dust of the dry woods on them made her look as though she'd be there forever: longer than they would.

His father made a sign to Dewey, and they got around Miss Hattie there and went on.

"This is where I had in mind the whole time," he said.

It was where there was an old, unrailed, concrete bridge across the Little Muscadine. A good jump—an impossible jump—separated the bridge from land, for the Old Road—overgrown, but still coming through the trees this far—fell away into a sandy ravine when it got to the river. The bridge stood out there high on its single foot, like a table in the water.

There was a sign, "Cross at Own Risk," and a plank limber as a hammock laid across to the bridge floor. Dewey ran the plank, ran the bridge's length, and gave a cry—it was an island.

The bearded trees hung in a ring around it all, the Little Muscadine without a sound threaded through the sand among fallen trees, and the two fishermen sat on the bridge, halfway across, baited their hooks from the can of worms taken out of a pocket, and hung their poles over the side.

They didn't catch anything, sure enough.

About noon, Dewey and his father stopped fishing and went into a lunch of biscuits and jelly the father took out of another pocket.

"This bridge don't belong to nobody," his father said, then. "It's just going begging. It's a wonder somebody don't stretch a tent over this good floor and live here, high and dry. You could have it clean to yourself. Know you could?"

"Me?" asked Dewey.

His father faintly smiled and ate a biscuit before he said, "You'd have to ask your ma about it first."

"There's another one!" said Dewey.

Another lady had dared to invade this place. Over the water and through the trees, on the same side of the river they'd come from, her face shone clear as a lantern light in nighttime. She'd found them.

"Blackie?" she called, and a white arm was lifted too. The sound was like the dove-call of April or May, and it carried as unsurely as something she had tried to throw them across that airy distance.

Blackie was his father's name, but he didn't answer. He sat just as he was, out in the open of the bridge, both knees pointed up blue, a biscuit with a bite gone out of it in his hand.

Then the lady turned around and disappeared into the trees.

Dewey could easily think she had gone off to die. Or if she hadn't, she would have had to die there. It was such a complaint she sent over, it was so sorrowful. And about what but death would ladies, anywhere, ever speak with such soft voices—then turn and run? Before she'd gone, the lady's face had been white and still as magic behind the trembling willow boughs that were the only bright-touched thing.

"I think she's gone," said Dewey, getting to his feet.

Turtles now lay on logs sticking up out of the low water, with their small heads raised. An old log was papped with baby turtles. Dewey counted fourteen, seven up one side and seven down the other. Just waiting for rain, said his father. On a giant log was a giant turtle, gray-tailed, the size of a dishpan, set at a laughable angle there, safe from everybody and everything.

With lunch over, they still didn't catch anything. And then the lady looked through the willow boughs again, in nearly the same place. She was giving them another chance.

She cupped her hands to her silent lips. She meant "Blackie!"

"Blackie!" There it was.

"You hold still," said his father. "She ain't calling you."

Nobody could hold so still as a man named Blackie.

That mysterious lady never breathed anything but the one word, and so softly then that it was all the word could do to travel over the water; still his father never said anything back, until she disappeared. Then he said, "Blackie yourself."

He didn't even bait his hook or say any longer what he would do to the fish if they didn't hurry up and change their minds. Yet when nothing came up on the hook, he looked down at his own son like a stranger cast away on this bridge from the long ago, before it got cut off from land.

Dewey baited his hook, and the first thing he knew he'd caught a fish.

"What is it, what is it?" he shouted.

"You got you a little goggle-eye there, son."

Dewey, dancing with it—it was six inches long and jumping on the hook—hugged his father's neck and said, "Well—ready to go?"

"No . . . Best not to stay either too long or too little-bit. I favor tarrying awhile," said his father.

Dewey sat back down, and gazed up at his father's solemn side-face—then followed the look his father shot across the river like a fishing line of great length, one that took hold.

Across the river the lady looked out for the third time. She was almost out of the willows now, on the sand. She put the little shells of her hands up to her throat. What did that mean? It was the way she'd pull her collar together if she'd been given a coat around her. It was about to rain. She knew as well as they did that people were looking at her hard; but she must not feel it, Dewey felt, or surely people would have to draw their looks away, and not fasten her there. She didn't have even one word to say, this time.

The bay tree that began moving and sighing over her head was the tall slender one Dewey had picked as his marker. With its head in a stroke of sun, it nodded like a silver flower. There was a little gentle thunder, and Dewey knew that her eyes shut, as well as he would know even in his sleep when his mother put down the windows in their house if a rain was coming. That way, she stood there and waited. And Dewey's father—whose sweat Dewey took a deep breath of as he stood up beside him—believed that the one *that* lady waited for was never coming over the bridge to her side, any more than she would come to his.

Then, with a little sound like a mouse somewhere in the world, a scratch, then a patter like many mice racing— and then at last the splash on Dewey's cheek—it simply began raining. Dewey looked all around—the river was dancing.

"Run now, son! Run for cover! It's fixing to pour down! I'll be right behind you!" shouted his father, running right past him and then jumping over the side of the bridge. Arms and legs spread wide as surprise itself he did a grand leap to the sand. But instead of sheltering under the bridge, he kept going, and was running up the bank now, toward Royals. Dewey resigned himself to go the same way. As for the lady, if she was still where they left her, about to disappear perhaps, she was getting wet.

They ran under the sounding trees and vines. It came down in earnest, feeling warm and cool together, a real spring shower.

"Trot under here!" called a pre-emptory voice.

"Miss Hattie! Forgot she was anywhere near," said Dewey's father, falling back. "Now we got to be nice to *her*."

"Good evening, Lavelle."

At that name, Dewey fell back, but his father went on. Maybe he was getting used to being called, today, and it didn't make any difference what name he got, by now.

Something as big as a sail came out through the brambles.

"Did you hear me?" said Miss Hattie—there she stood. "Get you both under this umbrella. I'm going straight back to town, and I'll take you with me. Can't take your fishing poles, unless you drag 'em."

"Yes'm," they said, and got under.

Starting forward, Miss Hattie held her own umbrella, a man with her or not, branches of trees coming or not, and the harder the rain fell the more energetically she held to the handle. There were little cowlicks of damp standing up all around the black fur of her collar. Her spectacles were on her nose, and both windows had drops all over them like pearls. Miss Hattie's coat tapered up like one tent, and the umbrella spread down like another one. They marched abreast or single file, as the lay of the land allowed, but always politely close together under the umbrella, either despising paths or taking a path so fragrant and newly slick it didn't seem familiar. But there was an almost forgotten landmark of early morning, boarded twin towers of a colored church, set back closet-like in the hanging moss. Dewey thought he knew where he was. Suddenly frogs from everywhere let loose on the world, as if they'd been wound up.

In no time, Miss Hattie brought them to the edge of the woods. Next they were at the gravel road and walking down the middle of it. The turn was coming where Royals could be seen spread out from Baptist church to schoolhouse.

Dewey, keeping watch around Miss Hattie's skirt, saw the lady appear in the distance behind them, running like a ghost across the road in the shining rain—shining, for the sun had looked through.

"The Devil is beating his wife," said Miss Hattie in a professional voice.

There ran the figure that the rain sheathed in a spinning cocoon of light—as if it ran in peril. It was cutting across Mr. Jep Royal's yard, where the Royals were all sitting inside the house and some cows as black as blackbirds came close and watched her go.

"Look at that, to the side," said Miss Hattie suddenly. "Who's that, young eyes?"

Dewey looked shyly under her forward sleeve and asked his father, "Reckon it's the lady?"

"Well, *call* her," said Miss Hattie. "Whoever she is, she can trot under this umbrella just as easy as we can. It's good size."

"La-dy!"

That was Dewey, hollering.

They stood and waited for the lady to come across the pasture, though his father looked very black, trapped under the umbrella. Had Miss Hattie looked at him, that showed what his name was and how he got it.

But the lady, now opposite, in a whole field of falling light, was all but standing still. Starting here, starting there, wavering, retreating, she made no headway at all. Then abruptly she disappeared into the Royals' pear orchard—this time for good.

"Maybe somebody new has escaped from the lunatic asylum," said Miss Hattie. "March."

On they went in the rain.

Opal Purcell slipped sideways through the elderberry bushes at the creek bank, with both hands laid, like a hat, on top of her head, and waited for them.

"Why, it's only my own niece," said Miss Hattie. "Trot under here, Opal. How do you like this rain?"

"Hey, Aunt Hat. Hey," said Opal to Dewey.

She was grown. Sometimes she waited on people in the Seed & Feed. She was plump as ever. She didn't look far enough around her aunt to speak to his father.

Miss Hattie touched Opal on the head. "Has it rained that much?" she said in a gratified way.

"I thought I saw you in the post office, Aunt Hat," objected Opal.

"I expect you did. I had the mail to tie up. I'm a fast worker when the case demands."

They were all compelled, of course, to keep up with Miss Hattie and stay with her and be company all the way back to town. Her black cotton umbrella lacked very little of being big enough for four, but it lacked some. Dewey gave Opal his place.

He marched ahead of them, still in step with his father, but out in the open rain, with his fish now let up high on its pole behind him. He felt the welcome plastering down of his hair on his forehead, and the relentless way the raindrops hit and bounced on him.

Opal Purcell had a look, to Dewey, as if she didn't know whether she was getting wet or not. It was his father's fishing look. And Miss Hattie's rainmaking look. He was the only one—out here in the rain itself—that didn't have it.

Like a pretty lady's hand, to tilt his face up a little and make him smile, deep satisfaction, almost love came down and touched him.

"Miss Hattie," he turned walking and said over his shoulder, "I caught me a goggle-eye perch back yonder, see him? I wish I could give him to you—for your supper!"

"You good and wet, honey?" she said back, marching there in the middle.

The brightest thing in Royals—rain was the loudest, on all the tin roofs—was the empty school bus drawn up under the shed of the filling station. The movie house, high up on its posts, was magnesia-bottle blue. Three red hens waited on the porch. Dewey's and Opal's eyes together looked out of their corners at the "Coming Saturday" poster of the charging white horse. But Miss Hattie didn't dismiss them at the movie house.

They passed the Baptist church getting red as a rose, and the Methodist church getting streaky. In the middle of the first crossing, the water tank stood and they walked under; water from its bottom, black and cold as ice, fell a drop for each head as always. And they passed along the gin, which alone would sleep the spring out. All around were the well-known ditches and little gullies; there were the chinaberry trees, and some Negroes and some dogs underneath them; but it all looked like some different place to Dewey—not Royals. There was a line of faces under the roof of the long store porch, but they looked, white and black, like the faces of new people. Nevertheless, all spoke to Miss Hattie, Blackie, Opal, and Dewey by name; and from their umbrella—out in the middle of the road, where it was coming down hardest—Miss Hattie did the speaking back.

"It's the beginning!" she called. "I'd a heap rather see it come this way than in torrents!"

"We're real proud of you, Miss Hattie!"

"You're still a credit to Royals, Miss Hattie!"

"Don't you drown yourself out there!"

"Oh, I won't," said Miss Hattie.

At the bank corner, small spotty pigs belonging to nobody, with snouts as long as corncobs, raced out in a company like clowns with the Circus, and ran with Dewey and Miss Hattie and all, for the rest of the way. There was one more block, and that was where the post office was. Also the Seed & Feed, and the schoolhouse beyond, and the Stave Mill Road; and also home was that way.

"Well, good-by, everybody," said Miss Hattie, arrived at the post office tree.

Dewey's father—the darkest Coker of the family, much

darker than Uncle Lavelle, who had run off a long time
ago, by Dewey's reckoning—bowed himself out backwards
from under the umbrella and straightened up in the rain.

"Much obliged for the favor, Miss Hattie," he said.
With a quiet hand he turned over his fishing pole to
Dewey, and was gone.

"Thank you, ma'am, I enjoyed myself," said Dewey.

"You're wet as a drowned rat," said Miss Hattie ad-
miringly.

Up beyond, the schoolhouse grew dim behind its silver
yard. The bell mounted at the gate was making the sound
of a bucket filling.

"I'll leave you with the umbrella, Opal. Opal, run
home," said Miss Hattie, pointing her finger at Opal's
chest, "and put down the south windows, and bring in
the quilts and dry them out again before the fire. I can't
tell you why I forgot clean about my own windows. You
might stand on a chair and find a real pretty quart of
snapbeans and put them on with that little piece of meat
out of the safe. Run now. Where've you been?"

"Nowheres.—Hunting poke salad," said Opal, making
a little face twice. She had wet cheeks, and there was a
blue violet in her dress, hanging down from a buttonhole,
and no coat on her back of any kind.

"Then dry yourself," said Miss Hattie. "*What's that?*"

"It's the train whistle," said Dewey.

Far down, the mail train crossed the three long trestles
over Little Muscadine swamp like knocking three knocks
at the door, and blew its whistle again through the rain.

Miss Hattie never let her powers interfere with mail
time, or mail time interfere with her powers. She had
everything worked out. She pulled open the door of her
automobile, right there. There on the back seat was her
mail sack, ready to go.

Miss Hattie lived next door—where Opal had now gone inside—and only used her car between here and the station; it stayed under the post office tree. Some day old Opal was going to take that car, and ride away. Miss Hattie climbed up inside.

The car roared and took a leap out into the rain. At the corner it turned, looking two stories high, swinging wide as Miss Hattie banked her curve, with a lean of her whole self deep to the right. She made it. Then she sped on the diagonal to the bottom of the hill and pulled up at the station just in time for Mr. Frierson to run out in his suspenders and hand the mail as the train rushed through. It hooked the old sack and flung off the new to Royals.

The rain slacked just a little on Miss Hattie while she hauled the mail uphill. Dewey stamped up the post office runway by her side to help her carry it in—the post office used to be a stable. He held the door open, they went inside, and the rain slammed down behind them.

"Dewey Coker?"

"Ma'am?"

"Why aren't you in school?"

In a sudden moment she dropped the sack and rubbed his head—just any old way—with something out of her purse; it might have been a dinner napkin. He rubbed cornbread crumbs as sharp as rocks out of his eye. Across the road, while this drying was happening, a wonderful white mule that had gotten into the cemetery and rolled himself around till he was green and white like a marble monument, got up to his feet and shivered and shook the raindrops everywhere.

"I may can still go," he said dreamily. "*Excalibur*—

"Nonsense! Don't you see that rain?" cried Miss Hattie. "You'll stay here in this post office till I tell you."

The post office inside was a long bare room that looked and smelled like a covered bridge, with only a little light at the other end where Miss Hattie's window was. Dewey had never stayed inside here more than a minute at a time, in his life.

"You make yourself at home," said Miss Hattie, and disappeared into the back.

Dewey stood the poles by the front door and kept his fish in his hand on the bit of line, while Miss Hattie put up the mail. After she had put it all up as she saw fit, then she gave it out: pretty soon here came everybody. There was a lot of conversation through the window.

"Sure is a treat, Miss Hattie! Only wish it didn't have to stop."

"It looks like a gully washer to me, Miss Hat!"

And someone leaned down and said to Dewey, "Hi, Dewey! I saw you! And what was *you* up to this evening?"

"It's a beginning," was all Miss Hattie would say. "I'll go back out there tomorrow, if I have the time, and if I live and don't nothing happen, and do some more on it. But depends on the size of the mail."

After everybody had shed their old letters and papers on the floor and tracked out, there would have been silence everywhere but for the bombardment on the roof. Miss Hattie still didn't come out of her little room back there, of which Dewey could see nothing but the reared-back honeycomb of her desk with nine letters in the holes.

Out here, motes danced lazily as summer flies in the running green light of the cracks in the walls. The hole of a missing stovepipe high up was blocked with a bouquet of old newspapers, yellow as roses. It was a little chilly. It smelled of rain, of fish, of pocket money and pockets. Whether the lonely dangling light was turned on or off it was hard to see. Its bulb hung down fierce in a little mask like a biting dog.

On the high table against the wall there was an ink well and a pen, as in a school desk, and an old yellow blotter limp as biscuit dough. Reaching tall, he rounded up the pen and with a great deal of the ink drew a picture on the blotter. He drew his fish. He gave it an eye and then mailed it through the slot to Miss Hattie.

Presently he hung his chin on the little ledge to her window, to see if she got it.

Miss Hattie was asleep in her rocking chair. She was sitting up with her head inclined, beside her little gas stove. She had laid away her hat, and there was a good weight to her hair, which was shaped and colored like the school bell. She looked noble, as if waiting to have the headsman chop off her head. All was quietness itself. For the rain had stopped. The only sound was the peeping of baby chicks from the parcel post at her feet.

"Can I go now?" he hollered.

"Mercy!" she exclaimed at once. "Did it bite? Nothing for you today! Who's that? I wasn't asleep! Whose face is that smiling at me? For pity's sakes!" She jumped up and shook her dress—some leaves fell out. Then she came to the window and said through it, "You want to go leave me? Run then! Because if you dream it's stopped, child, I won't be surprised a bit if it don't turn around and come back."

At that moment the post office shook with thunder, as if horses ran right through it.

Miss Hattie came to the door behind him. He slid down the runway with all he had. She remained there looking out, nodding a bit and speaking a few words to herself. All she had to say to him was "Trot!"

It was already coming down again, with the sound of

making up for the lapse that had just happened. As
Dewey began to run, he caught a glimpse of a patchwork
quilt going like a camel through the yard next door toward Miss Hattie's house. He supposed Opal was under
it. Fifteen years later it occurred to him it had very likely
been Opal in the woods.

Just in time, he caught and climbed inside the rolling
school bus with the children in it, and rode home after
all with the others, a sort of hero.

After the bus put him down, he ran cutting across under the charred pines. The big sky-blue violets his mother
loved were blooming, wet as cheeks. Pear trees were all
but in bloom under the purple sky. Branches were being
jogged with the rush and commotion of birds. The Cokers'
patch of mustard that had gone to seed shone like gold
from here. Dewey ran under the last drops, through the
hooraying mud of the pasture, and saw the corrugations
of their roof shining across it like a fresh pan of cornbread sticks. His father was off at a distance, on his knees
—back at mending the fences. Minnie Lee, Sue, and Annie
Bess were ready for Dewey and came flocking from the
door, with the baby behind on all fours. None of them
could hope to waylay him.

His mother stood in the back lot. Behind her, blue and
white, her morning wash hung to the ground, as wet as
clouds. She stood with a switch extended most strictly
over the head of the silky calf that drank from the old
brown cow—as though this evening she knighted it.

"Whose calf will that be? Mine?" he cried out to her.
It was to make her turn, but this time, he thought, her
answer would be yes.

"You have to ask your pa, son."

"Why do you always tell me the same thing? *Mama!*"

Arm straight before him, he extended toward her dear face his fish—still shining a little, held up by its tail, its eye and its mouth as agape as any big fish's. She turned.

"Get away from me!" she shrieked. "You and your pa! Both of you get the sight of you clear away!" She struck with her little green switch, fanning drops of milk and light. "Get in the house. Oh! If I haven't had enough out of you!"

Days passed—it rained some more, sometimes in the night—before Dewey had time to go back and visit the bridge. He didn't take his fishing pole, he just went to see about it. The sky had cleared in the evening, after school and the work at home were done with.

The river was up. It covered the sandbars and from the bridge he could no longer remember exactly how the driftwood had lain—only its upper horns stuck out of the water, where parades of brown bubbles were passing down. The gasping turtles had all dived under. The water must now be swimming with fish of all sizes and kinds.

Dewey walked the old plank back, there being no sand to drop down to. Then he visited above the bridge and wandered around in new places. They were drenched and sweet. The big fragrant bay was his marker.

He stood in the light of birdleg-pink leaves, yellow flower vines, and scattered white blooms each crushed under its drop of water as under a stone, the maples red as cinnamon drops and the falling, thready nets of willows, and heard the lonesomest sound in creation, an unknown bird singing through the very moment when he was the one that listened to it. Across the Little Muscadine the golden soldier-tassels of distant oaks filled with light, and there the clear sun dropped.

Before he got out of the river woods, it was nearly first-dark. The sky was pink and blue. The great moon had slid up in it, but not yet taken light, like the little plum tree that had sprung out in flower below. At that mysterious colored church, the one with the two towers and the two privies to the rear, that stood all in darkness, a new friend sat straight up on the top church step. Head to one side, little red tongue hanging out, it was a little black dog, his whole self shaking and alive from tip to tip. He might be part of the church, that was the way he acted. On the other hand, there was no telling where he might have come from.

Yet he had something familiar about him too. He had a look on his little pointed face—for all he was black; and was it he, or she?—that reminded Dewey of Miss Hattie Purcell, when she stood in the door of the post office looking out at the rain she'd brought and remarking to the world at large: "Well, I'd say that's right persnickety."

Circe

Needle in air, I stopped what I was making. From the upper casement, my lookout on the sea, I saw them disembark and find the path; I heard that whole drove of mine break loose on the beautiful strangers. I slipped down the ladder. When I heard men breathing and sandals kicking the stones, I threw open the door. A shaft of light from the zenith struck my brow, and the wind let out my hair. Something else swayed my body outward.

"Welcome!" I said—the most dangerous word in the world.

Heads lifted to the smell of my bread, they trooped inside—and with such a grunting and frisking at their heels to the very threshold. Star-gazers! They stumbled on my polished floor, strewing sand, crowding on each other, sizing up the household for gifts (thinking already of sailing away), and sighted upwards where the ladder went, to the sighs of the island girls who peeped from the kitchen door. In the hope of a bath, they looked in awe at their hands.

I left them thus, and withdrew to make the broth.

With their tear-bright eyes they watched me come in with the great winking tray, and circle the room in a winding wreath of steam. Each in turn with a pair of black-nailed hands swept up his bowl. The first were trotting at my heels while the last still reached with their hands. Then the last drank too, and dredging their snouts from the bowls, let go and shuttled into the company.

That moment of transformation—only the gods really like it! Men and beasts almost never take in enough of the wonder to justify the trouble. The floor was swaying like a bridge in battle. "Outside!" I commanded. "No dirt is allowed in this house!" In the end, it takes phenomenal neatness of housekeeping to put it through the heads of men that they are swine. With my wand seething in the air like a broom, I drove them all through the door— twice as many hooves as there had been feet before—to join their brothers, who rushed forward to meet them now, filthily rivaling, but welcoming. What tusks I had given them!

As I shut the door on the sight, and drew back into my privacy—deathless privacy that heals everything, even the effort of magic—I felt something from behind press like the air of heaven before a storm, and reach like another wand over my head.

I spun round, thinking, O gods, it has failed me, it's drying up. Before everything, I think of my power. One man was left.

"What makes you think you're different from anyone else?" I screamed; and he laughed.

Before I'd believe it, I ran back to my broth. I had thought it perfect—I'd allowed no other woman to come near it. I tasted, and it was perfect—swimming with oysters from my reef and flecks of golden pork, redolent with leaves of bay and basil and rosemary, with the glass of island wine tossed in at the last: it has been my infallible recipe. Circe's broth: all the gods have heard of it and envied it. No, the fault had to be in the drinker. If a man remained, unable to leave that magnificent body of his, then enchantment had met with a hero. Oh, I know those prophecies as well as the back of my hand—only nothing is here to warn me when it is *now*.

The island girls, those servants I support, stood there in the kitchen and smiled at me. I threw kettle and all at their withering heels. Let them learn that unmagical people are put into the world to justify and serve the magical—not to smile at them!

I whirled back again. The hero stood as before. But his laugh had gone too, after his friends. His gaze was empty, as though I were not in it—I was invisible. His hand groped across the rushes of a chair. I moved beyond him and bolted the door against the murmurous outside. Still invisibly, I took away his sword. I sent his tunic away to the spring for washing, and I, with my own hands, gave him his bath. Then he sat and dried himself before the fire—carefully, the only mortal man on an island in the sea. I rubbed oil on his shadowy shoulders, and on the rope of curls in which his jaw was set. His rapt ears still listened to the human silence there.

"I know your name," I said in the voice of a woman, "and you know mine by now."

I took the chain from my waist, it slipped shining to the floor between us, where it lay as if it slept, as I came forth. Under my palms he stood warm and dense as a myrtle grove at noon. His limbs were heavy, braced like a sleep-walker's who has wandered, alas, to cliffs above the sea. When I passed before him, his arm lifted and barred my way. When I held up the glass he opened his mouth. He fell among the pillows, his still-open eyes two clouds stopped over the sun, and I lifted and kissed his hand.

It was he who in a burst of speech announced the end of day. As though the hour brought a signal to the wan-

derer, he told me a story, while the owl made comment
outside. He told me of the monster with one eye—he had
put out the eye, he said. Yes, said the owl, the monster
is growing another, and a new man will sail along to blind
it again. I had heard it all before, from man and owl. I
didn't want his story, I wanted his secret.

When Venus leaned at the window, I called him by
name, but he had talked himself into a dream, and his
dream had him fast. I now saw through the cautious herb
that had protected him from my broth. From the first,
he had found some way to resist my power. He must
laugh, sleep, ravish, he must talk and sleep. Next it would
be he must die. I looked an age into that face above the
beard's black crescent, the eyes turned loose from mine
like the statues' that sleep on the hill. I took him by the
locks of his beard and hair, but he rolled away with his
snore to the very floor of sleep—as far beneath my reach
as the drowned sailor dropped out of his, in the tale he
told of the sea.

I thought of my father the Sun, who went on his divine
way untroubled, ambitionless—unconsumed; suffering no
loss, no heroic fear of corruption through his constant
shedding of light, needing no story, no retinue to vouch
for where he has been—even heroes could learn of the
gods!

Yet I know they keep something from me, asleep and
awake. There exists a mortal mystery, that, if I knew
where it was, I could crush like an island grape. Only
frailty, it seems, can divine it—and I was not endowed
with that property. They live by frailty! By the moment!
I tell myself that it is only a mystery, and mystery is only
uncertainty. (There is no mystery in magic! Men are
swine: let it be said, and no sooner said than done.) Yet
mortals alone can divine where it lies in each other, can
find it and prick it in all its peril, with an instrument

made of air. I swear that only to possess that one, tri-
fling secret, I would willingly turn myself into a harm-
less dove for the rest of eternity!

When presently he leapt up, I had nearly forgotten he
would move again—as a golden hibiscus startles you, all
flowers, when you are walking in some weedy place apart.

Yes, but he would not dine. Dinner was carried in, but
he would not dine with me until I would undo that day's
havoc in the pigsty. I pointed out that his portion was
served in a golden bowl—the very copy of that bowl my
own father the Sun crosses back in each night after his
journey of the day. But he cared nothing for beauty that
was not of the world, he did not want the first taste of
anything new. He wanted his men back. In the end, it
was necessary for me to cloak myself and go down in the
dark, under the willows where the bones are hung to the
wind, into the sty; and to sort out and bring up his
friends again from their muddy labyrinth. I had to pass
them back through the doorway as themselves. I could not
skip or brush lightly over one—he named and counted.
Then he could look at them all he liked, staggering up
on their hind legs before him. Their jaws sank asthmati-
cally, and he cried, "Do you know me?"

"It's Odysseus!" I called, to spoil the moment. But with
a shout he had already sprung to their damp embrace.

Reunions, it seems, are to be celebrated. (I have never
had such a thing.) All of us feasted together on meat
and bread, honey and wine, and the fire roared. We heard
out the flute player, we heard out the story, and the fair-
haired sailor, whose name is now forgotten, danced on the
table and pleased them. When the fire was black, my servants came languishing from the kitchen, and all the way
up the ladder to the beds above they had to pull the
drowsy-kneed star-gazers, spilling laughter and songs all

the way. I could hear them calling away to the girls as they would call them home. But the pigsty was where they belonged.

Hand in hand, we climbed to my tower room. His cheeks were grave and his eyes black, put out with puzzles and solutions. We conversed of signs, omens, premonitions, riddles and dreams, and ended in fierce, cold sleep. Strange man, as unflinching and as wound up as I am. His short life and my long one have their ground in common. Passion is our ground, our island—do others exist?

His sailors came jumping down in the morning, full of themselves and stories. Preparing the breakfast, I watched them tag one another, run rough-and-tumble around the table, regaling the house. "What did *I* do? How far did *I* go with it?" and in a reckless reassurance imitating the sounds of pigs at each other's backs. They were certainly more winsome now than they could ever have been before; I'd made them younger, too, while I was about it. But tell me of one that appreciated it! Tell me one now who looked my way until I had brought him his milk and figs.

When he made his appearance, we devoured a god's breakfast—all, the very sausages, taken for granted. The kitchen girls simpered and cried that if this went on, we'd be eaten out of house and home. But I didn't care if I put the house under greater stress for this one mortal than I ever dreamed of for myself—even on those lonely dull mornings when mist wraps the island and hides every path of the sea, and when my heart is black.

But a stir was upon them all from the moment they rose from the table. Treading on their napkins, tracking the clean floor with honey, they deserted me in the house and collected, arms wound on each other's shoulders, to talk beneath the sky. There they were in a knot, with him in the center of it. He folded his arms and sank his golden weight on one leg, while every ear on the island listened. I stood in the door and waited.

He walked up and said, "Thank you, Circe, for the hospitality we have enjoyed beneath your roof."

"What is the occasion for a speech?" I asked.

"We are setting sail," he said. "A year's visit is visit enough. It's time we were on our way."

Ever since the morning Time came and sat on the world, men have been on the run as fast as they can go, with beauty flung over their shoulders. I ground my teeth. I raised my wand in his face.

"You've put yourself to great trouble for us. You may have done too much," he said.

"I undid as much as I did!" I cried. "That was hard."

He gave me a pecking, recapitulating kiss, his black beard thrust at me like a shoe. I kissed it, his mouth, his wrist, his shoulder, I put my eyes to his eyes, through which I saw seas toss, and to the cabinet of his chest.

He turned and raised an arm to the others. "Tomorrow."

The knot broke and they wandered apart to the shore. They were not so forlorn when they could eat acorns and trot quickly where they would go.

It was as though I had no memory, to discover how early and late the cicadas drew long sighs like the playing out of all my silver shuttles. Wasn't it always the time of greatest heat, the Dog Star running with the Sun? The sea the color of honey looked sweet even to the tongue, the salt and vengeful sea. My grapes had ripened all over again while we stretched and drank our wine, and I ordered the harvest gathered and pressed—but this wine, I made clear to the servants, was to store. Hospitality is one thing, but I must consider how my time is endless, how I shall need wine endlessly. They smiled; but magic is the tree, and intoxication is just the little bird that flies in it to sing and flies out again. But the wanderers were watching the sun and waiting for the stars.

Now the night wind was rising. I went my way over the house as I do by night to see if all is well and holding together. From the rooftop I looked out. I saw the vineyards spread out like wings on the hill, the servants' huts and the swarthy groves, the sea awake, and the eye of the black ship. I saw in the moonlight the dance of the bones in the willows. "Old, displeasing ones!" I sang to them on the wind. "There's another now more displeasing than you! Your bite would be sweeter to my mouth than the soft kiss of a wanderer." I looked up at Cassiopeia, who sits there and needs nothing, pale in her chair in the stream of heaven. The old Moon was still at work. "Why keep it up, old woman?" I whispered to her, while the lions roared among the rocks; but I could hear plainly the crying of birds nearby and along the mournful shore.

I swayed, and was flung backward by my torment. I believed that I lay in disgrace and my blood ran green, like the wand that breaks in two. My sight returned to me when I awoke in the pigsty, in the red and black aurora of flesh, and it was day.

They sailed from me, all but one.

The youngest—Elpenor was his name—fell from my roof. He had forgotten where he had gone to sleep. Drunk on the last night, the drunkest of them all—so as not to be known any longer as only the youngest—he'd gone to sleep on the rooftop, and when they called him, his step went off into air. I saw him beating down through the light with rosy fists, as though he'd never left his mother's side till then.

They all ran from the table as though a star had fallen. They stood or they crouched above Elpenor fallen in my yard, low-voiced now like conspirators—as indeed they were. They wept for Elpenor lying on his face, and for themselves, as *he* wept for them the day they came, when I had made them swine.

He knelt and touched Elpenor, and like a lover lifted him; then each in turn held the transformed boy in his arms. They brushed the leaves from his face, and smoothed his red locks, which were still in their tangle from his brief attempts at love-making and from his too-sound sleep.

I spoke from the door. "When you dig the grave for that one, and bury him in the lonely sand by the shadow of your fleeing ship, write on the stone: 'I died of love.'"

I thought I spoke in epitaph—in the idiom of man. But when they heard me, they left Elpenor where he lay, and ran. Red-limbed, with linens sparkling, they sped over the windy path from house to ship like a rainbow in the sun, like new butterflies turned erratically to sea. While he stood in the prow and shouted to them, they loaded the greedy ship. They carried off their gifts from me—all unappreciated, unappraised.

I slid out of their path. I had no need to see them set sail, knowing as well as if I'd been ahead of them all the way, the far and wide, misty and islanded, bright and indelible and menacing world under which they all must go. But foreknowledge is not the same as the last word.

My cheek against the stony ground, I could hear the swine like summer thunder. These were with me still, pets now, once again—grumbling without meaning. I rose to my feet. I was sickened, with child. The ground fell away before me, blotted with sweet myrtle, with high oak that would have given me a ship too, if I were not tied to my island, as Cassiopeia must be to the sticks and stars of her chair. We were a rim of fire, a ring on the sea. His ship was a moment's gleam on a wave. The little son, I knew, was to follow—follow and slay him. That was the story. For whom is a story enough? For the wanderers who will tell it—it's where they must find their strange felicity.

I stood on my rock and wished for grief. It would not come. Though I could shriek at the rising Moon, and she, so near, would wax or wane, there was still grief, that couldn't hear me—grief that cannot be round or plain or solid-bright or running on its track, where a curse could get at it. It has no heavenly course; it is like mystery, and knows where to hide itself. At last it does not even breathe. I cannot find the dusty mouth of grief. I am sure now grief is a ghost—only a ghost in Hades, where ungrateful Odysseus is going—waiting on him.

Kin

"Mingo?" I repeated, and for the first moment I didn't know what my aunt meant. The name sounded in my ears like *something* instead of *somewhere*. I'd been making a start, just a little start, on my own news when Rachel came in in her stately way with the letter.

My aunt was bridling daintily at the unopened envelope in her hand. "Of course you'll be riding out there Sunday, girls, and without me."

"Open it—what does she say now?" said Kate to her mother. "Ma'am? If Uncle Felix—"

"Uncle Felix! Is *he* still living?"

Kate went "Shh!"

But I had only arrived the day before yesterday; and we had of course had so much to catch up with, besides, necessarily, parties. They expected me to keep up in spite of being gone almost my whole life, except for visits—I was taken away from Mississippi when I was eight. I was the only one in Aunt Ethel's downstairs bedroom neither partially undressed nor, to use my aunt's word, "reclining."

"Of course he is," said Aunt Ethel, tearing open the envelope at once, and bringing out an old-fashioned "correspondence card" filled up on both sides with a sharp, jet-black hand, and reading the end. Uncle Felix was her uncle, only my great-uncle. "He is," she said to Kate.

"*Still* this, *still* that," murmured Kate, looking at me sidelong. She was up on the bed too. She leaned lightly across her mother, who was in pink negligée, read ahead of her for an instant, and plucked the last piece of the city candy I had brought from the big shell dish Rachel had seen fit to put it in.

Uncontrite, I rocked. However, I did see I must stop showing what might be too much exuberance in Aunt Ethel's room, since she was old and not strong, and take things more as they came. Kate and I were double first cousins, I was the younger, and neither married yet, but *I* was not going to be an old maid! I was already engaged up North; though I had not yet come to setting a date for my wedding. Kate, though, as far as I could tell, didn't have anybody.

My little aunt, for her heart's sake, had to lie propped up. There inside her tester bed she sometimes looked out as if, I thought, she were riding in some old-fashioned carriage or litter. Now she had drawn that card and its envelope both to her pillowed face. She was smelling them. Mingo, of course, was the home place. It was miles from anywhere, and I saw that she was not to go there any more.

"Look at the gilt edge," she said, shining it. "Isn't it *remarkable* about Sister Anne? I wonder what drawer she went into to find *that* to favor us with? . . . 'Had to drop—' watch?—no, 'water on his tongue—yesterday so he could talk . . . Must *watch* him—day and night,' underlined. *Poor* old man. She insists, you know, Dicey, that's what she does."

"Buzzard," said Kate.

"Who," I sighed, for I thought she had said "sister,"

and there was no sister at all left of my Aunt Ethel's. But my mind had wandered for a moment. It was two-thirty in the afternoon, after an enormous dinner at which we had had company—six girls, chattering almost like ready-made bridesmaids—ending with wonderful black, bitter, moist chocolate pie under mountains of meringue, and black, bitter coffee. We could hear Rachel now, off in the distance, peacefully dropping the iced-tea spoons into the silver drawer in the pantry.

In this little courthouse town, several hours by inconvenient train ride from Jackson, even the cut grass in the yards smelled different from Northern grass. (Even by evidence of smell, I knew that really I was a stranger in a way, still, just at first.) And the spring was so much farther advanced—the birds so busy you turned as you would at people as they plunged by. Bloom was everywhere in the streets, wistaria just ending, Confederate jasmine beginning. And down in the gardens!—they were deep colored as old rugs in the morning and evening shade. Everybody grew some of the best of everybody else's flowers; by the way, if you thank a friend for a flower, it will not grow for you. Everywhere we went calling, Kate brought me out saying, "Here she is! Got off the train talking, and hasn't stopped yet." And everywhere, the yawning, inconvenient, and suddenly familiar rooms were as deep and inviting and compelling as the yawning big roses opening and shattering in one day in the heating gardens. At night, the moths were already pounding against the screens.

Aunt Ethel and Kate, and everybody I knew here, lived as if they had never heard of anywhere else, even Jackson—in houses built, I could judge now as a grown woman and a stranger, in the local version of the 1880's—tall and spread out at the bottom, with porches, and winged all over with awnings and blinds. As children, Kate and I were brought up across the street from each other—they were her grandfather's and my grandmother's houses. From Aunt Ethel's front window I could see our chinaberry tree, which Mother had always wanted to cut down, standing in slowly realized bloom. Our old house was lived in now by a family named Brown, who were not very much, I gathered—the porch had shifted, and the screens looked black as a set of dominoes.

Aunt Ethel had gone back to the beginning of her note now. "Oh-oh. Word has penetrated even Mingo, Miss Dicey Hastings, that you're in this part of the world! The minute you reached Mississippi our little paper had that notice you laughed at, that was all about your mother and me and your grandmother, so of course there's repercussions from Sister Anne. 'Why didn't we tell her!' But honestly, she might be the remotest kin in the world, for all you know when you're well, but let yourself get to ailing, and she'd show up in Guinea, if that's where you were, and *stay*. Look at Cousin Susan, 'A year if need be' is the way she put it about precious Uncle Felix."

"She'll be coming to you next if you don't hush about her," said Kate, sitting bolt upright on the bed. She adored her mother, her family. What she had was company-excitement. And I guess I had trip-excitement—I giggled. My aunt eyed us and tucked the letter away.

"But who is she, pure and simple?" I said.

"You'd just better not let her *in*," said Aunt Ethel to Kate. "That's what. Sister Anne Fry, dear heart. Declares she's wild to lay eyes on you. I *should* have shown you the letter. Recalls your sweet manners toward your elders. Sunday's our usual day to drive out there, you remember, Dicey, but I'm inclined to think—I feel now —it couldn't be just your coming brought on this midweek letter. Uncle Felix was taken sick on Valentine's Day and she got there by Saturday. Katee, since you're not working this week—if you're going, you'd better go on today."

"Oh, curses!" cried Kate to me. Kate had told them at the bank she was not working while I was here. We had planned something.

"Mama, what is she?" asked Kate, standing down in her cotton petticoat with the ribbon run in. She was not as tall as I. "I may be as bad as Dicey but I don't intend to go out there today without you and not have her straight."

Aunt Ethel looked patiently upwards as if she read now from the roof of the tester, and said, "Well, she's a remote cousin of Uncle Felix's, to begin with. Your third cousin twice removed, and your Great-aunt Beck's half-sister, my third cousin once removed and my aunt's half-sister, Dicey's—"

"Don't tell me!" I cried. "I'm not that anxious to claim kin!"

"She'll claim you! She'll come visit you!" cried Kate.

"I won't be here long enough." I could not help my smiles.

"When your mother was alive and used to come bringing you, visits were different," said my Aunt Ethel. "She stayed long enough to make us believe she'd fully got here. There'd be time enough to have alterations, from Miss Mattie, too, and transplant things in the yard if it was the season, even start a hook-rug—do a morning glory, at least—even if she'd never really see the grand finale. . . . Our generation knew more how to visit, whatever else escaped us, not that I mean to criticize one jot."

"Mama, what do you *want?*" said Kate in the middle of the floor. "Let me get you something."

"I don't want a thing," said her mother. "Only for my girls to please themselves."

"Well then, tell me who it was that Sister Anne one time, long time ago, was going to marry and stood up in the church? And she was about forty years old!" Kate said, and lightly, excitedly, lifted my hat from where I'd dropped it down on the little chair some time, to her own head—bare feet, petticoat, and all. She made a face at me.

Her mother was saying, "Now *that* is beyond me at the moment, perhaps because it didn't come off. Though he was some kind of off-cousin, too, I seem to recall . . . I'll have it worked out by the time you girls get back from where you're going.—Very becoming, dear."

"Kate," I said, "I thought Uncle Felix was old beyond years when I was a child. And now *I'll* be old in ten years, and so will you. And he's still alive."

"He *was* old!" cried Kate. "He *was!*"

"Light somewhere, why don't you," said her mother.

Kate perched above me on the arm of my chair, and we gently rocked.

I said, "He had red roses on his suspenders."

"When did he ever take his coat off for you to see that?" objected my aunt. "The whole connection always went out there for *Sundays*, and he was a very strict gentleman all his life, you know, and made us be ladies out there, more even than Mama and Papa did in town."

"But I can't remember a thing about Sister Anne," I said. "Maybe she was too much of a lady."

"Foot," said my aunt.

Kate said in a prompting, modest voice, "She fell in the well."

I cried joyously, "And she came out! Oh, I remember

her fine! Mournful! Those old black drapey dresses, and plastered hair."

"That was just the way she looked when she came out of the well," objected Kate.

"Mournful isn't exactly the phrase," said my aunt.

"Plastered black hair, and her mouth drawn down, exactly like that aunt in the front illustration of your *Eight Cousins*," I told Kate. "I used to think that was who it was."

"You're so bookish," said my aunt flatly.

"This is where all the books *were!*"—and there were the same ones now, no more, no less.

"On purpose, I think she fell," continued Kate. "Knowing there were plenty to pull her out. That was her contribution to Cousin Eva's wedding celebrations, and snitching a little of *her* glory. You're joggling me the way you're rocking."

"There's such a thing as being unfair, Kate," said her mother. "I always say, *poor* Sister Anne."

"*Poor* Sister Anne, then."

"And I think Dicey just *thinks* she remembers it because she's heard it."

"Well, at least she had something to be poor about!" I said irrepressibly. "Falling in the well, and being an old maid, that's two things!"

Kate cried, "Don't rock so headlong!"

"Maybe she even knew what she was about. Eva's Archie Fielder got drunk every whipstitch for the rest of his life," said Aunt Ethel.

"Only tell me this, somebody, and I'll be quiet," I said. "What poor somebody's Sister Anne was she to begin with?"

Then I held the rocker and leaned against my cousin. I was terrified that I had brought up Uncle Harlan. Kate had warned me again how, ever since his death seventeen years ago, Aunt Ethel could not bear to hear the name of her husband spoken, or to speak it herself.

"Poor Beck's, of course," said Aunt Ethel. "She's a little bit kin on both sides. Since you ask, Beck's *half-sister*—that's why we were always so careful to call her Sister."

"Oh. I thought that was just for teasing," said Kate.

"Well, of course the teasing element is not to be denied," said Aunt Ethel.

"Who began—" My hat was set, not at all rightly, on my own head by Kate—like a dunce cap.

The town was so quiet the doves from the river woods could be heard plainly. In town, the birds were quiet at this hour. Kate and I went on bobbing slowly up and down together as we rocked very gently by Aunt Ethel's bed. I saw us in the pier glass across the room. Looking at myself as the visitor, I considered myself as having a great deal still waiting to confide. My lips opened.

"He was ever so courtly," said my aunt. "Nobody in the family more so."

Kate with a tiny sting pulled a little hair from my neck, where it has always grown too low. I slapped at her wrist.

"But this last spell when I couldn't get out, and he's begun failing, what I remember about him is what I used to be told as a child, isn't that strange? When I knew him all my life and loved him. For instance, that he was a great one for serenading as a young man."

"Serenading!" said Kate and I together, adoring her and her memory. "I didn't know he could sing," said Kate.

"He couldn't. But he *was* a remarkable speller," said my aunt. "A born speller. I remember how straight he stood when they called the word. You know the church out there, like everything else in the world, raised its money by spelling matches. He knew every word in the deck. One time—one time, though!—I turned Uncle Felix down. I was not so bad myself, child though I was. And it isn't . . ."

"Ma'am?"

"It just isn't fair to have water dropped on your tongue, is it!"

"She ought not to have told you, the old buzzard!"

"The word," said Aunt Ethel, "the word was knick-knack. K-n-i-c-k, knick, hyphen, k-n-a-c-k, knack, knick-knack."

"She only writes because she has nothing else to do, away out yonder in the country!"

"She used to get *dizzy* very easily," Aunt Ethel spoke out in a firm voice, as if she were just waking up from a nap. "Maybe she did well—maybe a girl might do well sometimes *not* to marry, if she's not cut out for it."

"Aunt Ethel!" I exclaimed. Kate, sliding gently off the arm of my chair, was silent. But as if I had said something more, she turned around, her bare foot singing on the matting, her arm turned above her head, in a saluting, mocking way.

"Find me her letter again, Kate, where is it?" said Aunt Ethel, feeling under her solitaire board and her pillow. She held that little gilt-edged card, shook it, weighed it, and said, "All that really troubles me is that I can't bear for her to be on Uncle Felix's hands for so long! He was always so courtly, and his family's all, all in the church-yard now (but us!)—or New York!"

"Mama, let me bring you a drink of water."

"Dicey, I'm going to *make* you go to Mingo."

"But I want to go!"

She looked at me uncomprehending. Kate gave her a

glass of water, with ice tinkling in it. "That reminds me, whatever you do, Kate, if you do go today, take that fresh Lady Baltimore cake out to the house—Little Di can sit and hold it while you drive. Poor Sister Anne can't cook and loves to eat. She can *eat* awhile. And make Rachel hunt through the shelves for some more green tomato pickle. Who'll put that up next year!"

"If you talk like that," said Kate, "we're going to go right this minute, right out into the heat. I thought this was going to be a good day."

"Oh, it is! Grand— Run upstairs both, and get your baths, you hot little children. You're supposed to go to Suzanne's, I know it." Kate, slow-motion, leaned over and kissed her mother, and took the glass. "Kate!—If only I could see him one more time. As he was. And Mingo. Old Uncle Theodore. The peace. Listen: you give him my love. He's *my* Uncle Felix. Don't tell him why I didn't come. That might distress him more than not seeing me there."

"What's Uncle Felix's trouble?" I asked, shyly at last: but things, even fatal things, did have names. I wanted to know.

Aunt Ethel smiled, looked for a minute as if she would not be allowed to tell me, and then said, "Old age.—I think Sister Anne's lazy, *idle!*" she cried. "You're drawing it out of me. She never cooked nor sewed nor even cultivated her mind! She was a lily of the field." Aunt Ethel suddenly showed us both highly polished little palms, with the brave gesture a girl uses toward a fortune teller —then looked into them a moment absently and hid them at her sides. "She just hasn't got anybody of her own, that's her trouble. And she needs somebody."

"Hush! She *will* be coming here next!" Kate cried, and our smiles began to brim once more.

"She has no inner resources," confided my aunt, and

watched to see if I were too young to guess what that meant. "How you girls do set each other off! Not that you're bothering me, I love you in here, and wouldn't deprive myself *of* it. Yes, you all just better wait and go Sunday. Make things as usual." She shut her eyes.

"Look—look!" chanted Kate.

Rachel, who believed in cutting roses in the heat of the day—and nobody could prevent her now, since we forgot to cut them ourselves or slept through the mornings—came in Aunt Ethel's room bearing a vaseful. Aunt Ethel's roses were at their height. A look of satisfaction on Rachel's face was like something nobody could interrupt. To our sighs, for our swooning attitudes, she paraded the vase through the room and around the bed, where she set it on the little table there and marched back to her kitchen.

"*Rachel* wants you to go. All right, you tell Uncle Felix," said Aunt Ethel, turning toward the roses, spreading her little hand out chordlike over them, "—of course he must have these—that *that's* Souvenir de Claudius Pernet—and *that's* Mermaid—Mary Wallace—Silver Moon—those three of course Étoiles—and oh, Duquesa de Penaranda—Gruss an Aachen's of course his cutting he grew for me a thousand years ago—but there's my Climbing Thor! Gracious!" she sighed, looking at it. Still looking at the roses she waited a moment. Pressing out of the vase, those roses of hers looked heavy, drunken with their own light and scent, their stems, just two minutes ago severed with Rachel's knife, vivid with pale thorns through cutglass. "You know, Sundays always *are* hotter than any other days, and I tell you what: I do think you'd better go on to Mingo today, regardless of what you find."

Circling around in her mind like old people—which

Aunt Ethel never used to do, she never used to get back!
—she got back to where she started.

"Yes'm," said Kate.

"Aunt Ethel, wouldn't it be better for everybody if he'd
come in town to the hospital?" I asked, with all my city
seriousness.

"He wouldn't consider it. So give Sister Anne my love,
and give Uncle Felix my dear love. Will you remember?
Go on, naked," said my aunt to her daughter. "Take your
cousin upstairs in her city bonnet. You both look right
feverish to me. Start in a little while, so you can get your
visit over and come back in the cool of the evening."

"These nights now are so bright," said my cousin Kate,
with a strange stillness in her small face, transfixed, as
if she didn't hear the end of the messages and did not
think who was listening to her either, standing with bare
arms pinned behind her head, with the black slick hair
pinned up, "these nights are so bright I don't mind, I
don't care, how long any ride takes, or how late I ever
get home!"

I jumped up beside her and said, pleadingly somehow,
to them both, "Do you know—I'd *forgotten* the Milky
Way!"

My aunt didn't see any use answering that either. But
Kate and I were suddenly laughing and running out together as if we were going to the party after all.

Before we set out, we tiptoed back into Aunt Ethel's
room and made off with the roses. Rachel had darkened
it. Again I saw us in the mirror, Kate pink and me blue,
both our dresses stiff as boards (I had gone straight into
Kate's clothes) and creaking from the way Rachel starched
them, our teeth set into our lips, half-smiling. I had tried
my hat, but Kate said, "Leave that, it's entirely too grand

for out there, didn't you hear Mama?" Aunt Ethel stayed motionless, and I thought she was bound to look pretty, even asleep. I wasn't quite sure she was asleep.

"Seems mean," said Kate, looking between the horns of the reddest rose, but I said, "She meant us to."

"Negroes always like them full blown," said Kate.

Out in the bright, "Look! Those crazy starlings have come. They always pick the greenest day!" said Kate.

"Well, maybe because they look so pretty in it," I said. There they were, feeding all over the yard and every yard, iridescently black and multiplied at our feet, bound for the North. Around the house, as we climbed with our loads into the car, I saw Rachel looking out from the back hall window, with her cheek in her hand. She watched us go, carrying off her cake and her flowers too.

I was thinking, if I always say "still," Kate still says "always," and laughed, but would not tell her.

Mingo, I learned, was only nine miles and a little more away. But it was an old road, in a part the highway had deserted long ago, lonely and winding. It dipped up and down, and the hills felt high, because they were bare of trees, but they probably weren't very high—this was Mississippi. There was hardly ever a house in sight.

"So green," I sighed.

"Oh, but poor," said Kate, with her look of making me careful of what I said. "Gone to pasture now."

"Beautiful to me!"

"It's clear to Jericho. Looks like that cake would set heavy on your knees, in that old tin Christmas box."

"I'm not ever tired in a strange place. Banks and towers of honeysuckle hanging over that creek!" We crossed an iron bridge.

"That's the Hushomingo River."

We turned off on a still narrower, bumpier road. I began to see gates.

Near Mingo, we saw an old Negro man riding side saddle, except there was no saddle at all, on a slow black horse. He was coming to meet us—that is, making his way down through the field. As we passed, he saluted by holding out a dark cloth cap stained golden.

"Good evening, Uncle Theodore," nodded Kate. She murmured, "Rachel's his daughter, did you know it? But she never comes back to see him."

I sighed into the sweet air.

"Oh, Lordy, we're too late!" Kate exclaimed.

On the last turn, we saw cars and wagons and one yellow wooden school bus standing empty and tilted to the sides up and down the road. Kate stared back for a moment toward where Uncle Theodore had been riding so innocently away. Primroses were blowing along the ditches and between the wheelspokes of wagons, above which empty cane chairs sat in rows, and some of the horses were eating the primroses. That was the only sound as we stood there. No, a chorus of dogs was barking in a settled kind of way.

From the gate we could look up and see the house at the head of the slope. It looked right in size and shape, but not in something else—it had a queer intensity for afternoon. Was every light in the house burning? I wondered. Of course: very quietly out front, on the high and sloping porch, standing and sitting on the railing between the four remembered, pale, square cypress posts, was stationed a crowd of people, dressed darkly, but vaguely powdered over with the golden dust of their thick arrival here in mid-afternoon.

Two blackly spherical Cape Jessamine bushes, old presences, hid both gateposts entirely. Such old bushes bloomed fantastically early and late so far out in the country, the way they did in old country cemeteries.

"The whole countryside's turned out," said Kate, and gritted her teeth, the way she did last night in her sleep.

What I could not help thinking, as we let ourselves through the gate, was that I'd either forgotten or never known how *primitive* the old place was.

Immediately my mind remembered the music box up there in the parlor. It played large, gilt-like metal discs, pierced with holes—eyes, eyelids, slits, mysterious as the symbols in a lady's dress pattern, but a whole world of them. When the disc was turned in the machine, the pattern of holes unwound a curious, metallic, depthless, cross music, with silences clocked between the notes. Though I did not like especially to hear it, I used to feel when I was here I must beg for it, as you should ask an old lady how she is feeling.

"I hate to get there," said Kate. She cried, "What a welcome for you!" But I said, "Don't say that." She fastened that creaky gate. We trudged up the straight but uneven dirt path, then the little paved walk toward the house. We shifted burdens, Kate took the cake and I took the flowers—the roses going like headlights in front of us. The solemnity on the porch was overpowering, even at this distance. It was serene, imperturbable, gratuitous: it was of course the look of "good country people" at such times.

On either side of us were Uncle Felix's roses—hillocks of bushes set in hillocks of rank grass and ragged-robins, hung with roses the size of little biscuits; indeed they already had begun to have a baked look, with little carmine edges curled. Kate dipped on one knee and came up with a four-leaf clover. She could always do that, even now, even carrying a three-layer cake.

By the house, wistaria had taken the scaffolding where a bell hung dark, and gone up into a treetop. The wistaria trunk, sinews raised and twined, like some old thigh, rose above the porch corner, above roof and all, where its sheet of bloom, just starting to go, was faded as an old sail. In spite of myself, I looked around the corner for that well: there it was, squat as a tub beneath the overpiece, a tiger-cat asleep on its cover.

The crowd on the porch were men and women, mostly old, some young, and some few children. As we approached they made no motion; even the young men sitting on the steps did not stand up. Then an old man came out of the house and a lady behind him, the old man on canes and the lady tiptoeing. Voices were murmuring softly all around.

Viewing the body, I thought, my breath gone—but nobody here's kin to me.

The lady had advanced to the head of the steps. It had to be Sister Anne. I saw her legs first—they were old—and her feet were set one behind the other, like an "expression teacher's," while the dress she had on was rather girlish, black taffeta with a flounce around it. But to my rising eyes she didn't look half so old as she did when she was pulled back out of the well. Her hair was not black at all. It was rusty brown, soft and unsafe in its pins. She didn't favor Aunt Ethel and Mama and them, or Kate and me, or any of us in the least, I thought—with that short face.

She was beckoning—a gesture that went with her particular kind of uncertain smile.

"What do I see? Cake!"

She ran down the steps. I bore down on Kate's shoulder behind her. Ducking her head, Kate hissed at me. What had I said? "Who pulled her out?"?

"You *surprised* me!" Sister Anne cried at Kate. She took the cake box out of her hands and kissed her. Two spots of red stabbed her cheeks. I was sorry to observe that the color of her hair was the very same I'd been noticing that spring in robins' breasts, a sort of stained color.

"Long-lost cousin, ain't you!" she cried at me, and gave me the same kiss she had given Kate—a sort of reprisal-kiss. Those head-heavy lights of Aunt Ethel's roses smothered between our unequal chests.

"Monkeys!" she said, leading us up, looking back and forth between Kate and me, as if she had to decide which one she liked best, before anything else in the world could be attended to. She had a long neck and that short face, and round, brown, jumpy eyes with little circles of wrinkles at each blink, like water wrinkles after something's popped in; that looked somehow like a twinkle, at her age. "Step aside for the family, please?" she said next, in tones I thought rather melting.

Kate and I did not dare look at each other. We did not dare look anywhere. As soon as we had moved through the porch crowd and were arrived inside the breezeway —where, however, there were a few people too, standing around—I looked and saw the corner clock was wrong. I was deeply aware that all clocks worked in this house, as if they had been keeping time just for me all this while, and I remembered that the bell in the yard was rung every day at straight-up noon, to bring them in out of the fields at picking time. And I had once supposed they rang it at midnight too.

Around us, voices sounded as they always did everywhere, in a house of death, soft and inconsequential, and tidily assertive.

"I believe Old Hodge's mules done had an attack of

the wanderlust. Passed through my place Tuesday headed
East, and now you seen 'em in Goshen."

Sister Anne was saying bodingly to us, "You just come
right on *through*."

This was where Kate burst into tears. I held her to
me, to protect her from more kisses. "When, when?" she
gasped. "When did it happen, Sister Anne?"

"Now when did what happen?"

That was the kind of answer one kind of old maid loves
to give. It goes with "Ask me sometime, and I'll tell you."
Sister Anne lifted her brow and fixed her eye on the parlor doorway. The door was opened into that room, but
the old red curtain was drawn across it, with bright light,
looking red too, streaming out around it.

Just then there was a creaking sound inside there, like
an old winter suit bending at the waist, and a young
throat was cleared.

"Little bit of commotion here today, but I *would* rather
you didn't tell Uncle Felix anything about it," said Sister
Anne.

"Tell him! Is he alive?" Kate cried wildly, breaking
away from me, and then even more wildly, "I might have
known it! What sort of frolic are you up to out here,
Sister Anne?"

Sister Anne suddenly marched to the other side of us
and brought the front bedroom door to with a good country slam. That room—Uncle Felix's—had been full of
people too.

"I beg your pardon," said Kate in a low voice in the
next moment. We were still just inside the house—in the
breezeway that was almost as wide as the rooms it ran
between from front porch to back. It was a hall, really,
but still when I was a child called the breezeway. Open

at the beginning, it had long been enclosed, and papered like the parlor, in red.

"Why, Kate. You all would be the first to *know*. Do you think I'd have let everybody come, regardless of promises, if Uncle Felix had chosen *not* to be with us still, on the day?"

While we winced, a sudden flash filled the hall with light, changing white to black, black to white—I saw the roses shudder and charge in my hands, Kate with white eyes rolled, and Sister Anne with the livid brow of a hostess and a pencil behind one ear.

"That's what you mean," said Sister Anne. "That's a photographer. He's here in our house today, taking pictures. He's *itinerant*," she said, underlining in her talk. "And he *asked* to use our parlor—we didn't ask *him*. Well —it *is* complete."

"What is?"

"Our parlor. And all in shape—curtains washed—*you know*."

Out around the curtain came the very young man, dressed in part in a soldier's uniform not his, looking slightly dazed. He tiptoed out onto the porch. The bedroom door opened on a soft murmuring again.

"Listen," said Sister Anne, leaning toward it. "Hear them in yonder?"

A voice was saying, "My little girl says she'd rather have come on this trip than gone to the zoo."

There was a look on Sister Anne's face as fond and startling as a lover's. Then out the door came an old lady with side-combs, in an enormous black cotton dress. An old man came out behind her, with a mustache discolored like an old seine. Sister Anne pointed a short strict finger at them.

"We're together," said the old man.

"I've got everything under control," Sister Anne called over her shoulder to us, leaving us at once. "Luckily, I was always able to be in two places at the same time, so I'll be able to visit with you back yonder and keep things moving up front, too. Now, what was your name, sir?"

At the round table in the center of the breezeway, she leaned with the old man over a ledger opened there, by the tray of glasses and the water pitcher.

"But where could Uncle Felix be?" Kate whispered to me. As for me, I was still carrying the roses.

Sister Anne was guiding the old couple toward the curtain, and then she let them into the parlor.

"Sister Anne, where have you got him put?" asked Kate, following a step.

"You just come right on through," Sister Anne called to us. She said, behind her hand, "They've left the fields, dressed up like Sunday and Election Day put together, but I can't say they all stopped long enough to bathe, ha-ha! April's a pretty important time, but having your picture taken beats that! Don't have a chance of that out this way more than once or twice in a lifetime. Got him put back out of all the commotion," she said, leading the way. "The photographer's name is—let me see. He's of the Yankee persuasion, but that don't matter any longer, eh, Cousin Dicey? But I shouldn't be funny. Anyway, traveled all the way from some town somewhere since *February*, he tells me. Mercy, but it's hot as churchtime up there, with 'em so packed in! Did it ever occur to you how vain the human race can be if you just give 'em a chance?"

There was that blinding flash again—curtain or not, it came right around it and through it, and down the hall.

"Smells like gunpowder," said Kate stonily.

"Does," agreed Sister Anne. She looked flattered, and said, "May *be*."

"I feel like a being from another world," I said all at once, just to the breezeway.

"Come on, then," said Sister Anne. "Kate, leave her alone. Oh, Uncle Felix'll eat you two little boogers up."

Not such small haunches moved under that bell-like skirt; the skirt's hem needed mending where a point hung down. Just as I concentrated and made up my mind that Sister Anne weighed a hundred and forty-five pounds and was sixty-nine years old, she mounted on tiptoe like a little girl, and I had to bite my lip to keep from laughing. Kate was steering me by the elbow.

"Now how could she have *moved* him away back here," Kate marveled. Her voice might even have been admiring, with Sister Anne not there.

"Hold your horses while I look at this cake," said Sister Anne, turning off at the kitchen. "What I want to see is *what kind*."

She squealed as if she had seen a mouse. She took a lick of the icing on her finger before she covered the cake again and set it on the table. "My favorite. And how is Cousin Ethel?" Then she reached for my roses.

"Your ring!" she cried—a cry only at the last second subdued. "Your ring!"

She took my face between her fingers and thumb and shook my cheeks, as though I could not hear what she said at all. She could do this because we were kin to each other.

With unscratchable hands she began sticking the roses into a smoky glass vase too small for them, into which she'd run too little water. Of course there was plumbing. The well was abandoned.

"Well," she said, poking in the flowers, as though sud-

denly we had all the time in the world, "the other morning, I was looking out at the road, and along came a
dusty old-time Ford with a trunk on the back, real slow,
then stopped. Was a man. I wondered. And in a minute,
knock knock knock. I changed my shoes and went to the
door with my finger to my lips." She showed us.

"He was still there, on the blazing porch—eleven-fif-
teen. He was a middle-age man all in hot black, short,
but reared back, like a stove handle. He gave me a calling card with a price down in the corner, and leaned in
and whispered he'd like to use the parlor. He was an
itinerant! That's almost but not quite the same thing as
a Gypsy. I hadn't seen a living person in fourteen days,
except here, and he was an itinerant photographer with
a bookful of orders to take pictures. I made him open
and show me his book. It was chock-full. All kinds of
names of all kinds of people from all over everywhere.
New pages clean, and old pages scratched out. In purple,
indelible pencil. I flatter myself I *don't get* lonesome, but
I felt sorry for *him*.

"I first told him he had taken me by surprise, and then
thanked him for the compliment, and then said, after persuasion like that, he *could* use the parlor, *providing* he
would make it quiet, because my cousin here wasn't up
to himself. And he assured me it was the quietest profes-
sion on earth. That he had chosen it because it *was* such
quiet, refined work, and also so he could see the world
and so many members of the human race. I said I was
a philosopher too, only I thought the sooner the better,
and we made it today. And he borrowed a bucket of water
and poured it steaming down the radiator, and returned
the bucket, and was gone. I almost couldn't believe he'd
been here.

"Then here today, right after dinner, in they start

pouring. There's more people living in and around Mingo community than you can shake a stick at, more than you would ever dream. Here they come, out of every little high road and by road and cover and dell, four and five and six at the time—draw up or hitch up down at the foot of the hill and come up and shake hands like Sunday visitors. Everybody that can walk, and two that can't. I've got one preacher out there brought by a delegation. Oh, it's like Saturday and Sunday put together. The rounds the fella must have made! It's not as quiet as all he said, either. There's those mean little children, he never said a word about them, the spook.

"So I said all right, mister, I'm ready for you. I'll show them where they can sit and where they can wait, and I'll call them. I says to them, 'When it's not your turn, please don't get up. If you want anything, ask me.' And I told them that any that had to, could smoke, but I wasn't ready to have a fire today, so mind out.

"And he took the parlor right over and unpacked his suitcase, and put up his lights, and unfolded a camp stool, until he saw the organ bench with the fringe around it. And shook out a big piece of scenery like I'd shake out a bedspread and hooked it to the wall, and commenced pouring that little powder along something like a music stand. "First!" he says, and commenced calling them in. I took over that. He and I go by his book and take them in order one at a time, all fair, honest, and above-board."

"And so what about Uncle Felix!" cried Kate, as if now she had her.

"The niggers helped, to get him back there, but it was mostly my fat little self," said Sister Anne. "Oh, you mean how come he consented? I expect I told him a story." She led us back to the hall, where a banjo hung like a stopped clock, and some small, white-haired children were marching to meet each other, singing "Here Comes the Duke A-Riding, Riding," in flat, lost voices. I too used to think that breezeway was as long as a tunnel through some mountain.

"Get!" said Sister Anne, and clapped her hands at them. They flung to the back, off the back porch into the sun and scattered toward the barn. With reluctance I observed that Sister Anne's fingers were bleeding from the roses. Off in the distance, a herd of black cows moved in a light of green, the feathery April pastures deep with the first juicy weeds of summer.

There was a small ell tacked onto the back of the house, down a turn of the back porch, leading, as I knew, to the bathroom and the other little room behind that. A young woman and little boy were coming out of the bathroom.

"Look at that," shuddered Sister Anne. "Didn't take them long to find out what *we've* got."

I never used to think that back room was to be taken seriously as part of the house, because apples were kept in it in winter, and because it had an untrimmed, flat board door like a shed door, where you stuck your finger through a rough hole to lift up the latch.

Sister Anne stuck in her finger, opened the door, and we all three crowded inside the little room, which was crowded already.

Uncle Felix's side and back loomed from a featherbed, on an old black iron frame of a bedstead, which tilted downwards toward the foot with the sinking of the whole house from the brow of the hill toward the back. He sat white-headed as one of those escaping children, but not childlike—a heavy bulk, motionless, in a night-shirt, facing the window. A woven cotton spread was about his knees. His hands, turned under, were lying one on each side of him, faded from outdoor burn, mottled amber and silver.

"That's a nigger bed," said Kate, in one tone, one word. I turned and looked straight into her eyes.

"*It—is—not*," said Sister Anne. Her whole face shook, as if Kate could have made it collapse. Then she bowed her head toward us—that we could go on, now, if that was the spirit we had come in.

"Good evening, sir," said Kate, in a changed voice.

I said it after her.

Uncle Felix's long, mute, grizzly head poked around his great shoulder and, motionless again, looked out at us. He visited this gaze a long time on a general point among the three different feminine faces—if you could call Sister Anne's wholly feminine—but never exactly on any of them. Gradually something left his eyes. Conviction was what I missed. Then even that general focus altered as though by a blow, a rap or a tap from behind, and his old head swung back. Again he faced the window, the only window in the house looking shadeless and shameless to the west, the glaring west.

Sister Anne bore the roses to the window and set them down on the window sill in his line of sight. The sill looked like the only place left where a vase could safely be set. Furniture, odds and ends, useless objects were everywhere, pushed by the bed even closer together. There were trunks, barrels, chairs with the cane seats hanging in a fringe. I remembered how sometimes in winter, dashing in here where the window then blew icily upon us, we would snatch an apple from the washed heap on the floor and run slamming out before we would freeze to death; that window always stayed open, then as now propped with a piece of stovewood. The walls were still rough boards with cracks between. Dust had come in everywhere,

rolls of dust or lint or cottonwood fuzz hung even from
the ceiling, glinting like everything else in the unfair
light. I was afraid there might be dirt-daubers' nests if
I looked. Our roses glared back at us as garish as anything living could be, almost like paper flowers, a magician's bouquet that had exploded out of a rifle to shock
and amaze us.

"We'll enjoy our sunset from over the pasture this evening, won't we, Uncle Felix!" called Sister Anne, in a
loud voice. It was the urgent opposite of her conspira-
torial voice. "I bet we're fixing to have a gorgeous one
—it's so dusty! You were saying last week, Cousin Felix,
we already need a rain!"

Then to my amazement she came and rested her foot
on a stack of mossy books by the bed—I was across from
her there—and leaned her elbow on her lifted knee, and
looked around the room with the face of a brand-new visitor. I thought of a prospector. I could look if she could.
What must have been a Civil War musket stood like a
forgotten broom in the corner. On the coal bucket sat an
old bread tray, split like a melon. There was even a dress
form in here, rising among the trunks, its inappropriate
bosom averted a little, as though the thing might still be
able to revolve. If it were spanked, how the dust would
fly up!

"Well, he's not going to even know *me* today," said
Sister Anne, teasing me. "Well! I mustn't stay away too
long at a time. Excuse me, Uncle Felix! I'll be right
back," she said, taking down her tomboy foot. At the
door she turned, to look as us sadly.

Kate and I looked at each other across the bed.

"Isn't this just—like—her!" said Kate with a long
sigh.

As if on second thought she pulled open the door sud-

denly and looked off after her. From the other part of
the house came the creakings of that human tiptoeing and
passing going on in the breezeway. A flash of light traveled around the bend. Very close by, a child cried. Kate
shut the door.

Back came Sister Anne—she really was back in a
minute. She looked across at me. "Haven't you spoken?
Speak! Tell him who you are, child! What did you come
for?"

Instead—without knowing I was going to do it—I
stepped forward and my hand moved out of my pocket
with my handkerchief where the magnolia-fuscata flowers
were knotted in the corner, and I put it under Uncle
Felix's heavy brown nose.

He opened his mouth. I drew the sweet handkerchief
back. The old man said something, with dreadful diffi-
culty.

"Hide," said Uncle Felix, and left his mouth open with
his tongue out for anybody to see.

Sister Anne backed away from us all and kept backing, to the front of the paper-stuffed fireplace, as if she
didn't even know the seasons. I almost expected to see
her lift her skirt a little behind her. She gave me a playful look instead.

"Hide," said Uncle Felix.

We kept looking at her. Sister Anne gave a golden,
listening smile, as golden as a Cape Jessamine five days
old.

"Hide," gasped the old man—and I made my first
movement. "And I'll go in. Kill 'em all. I'm old enough
I swear you Bob. Told you. Will for sure if you don't
hold me, hold me."

Sister Anne winked at me.

"Surrounded . . . They're inside." On this word he

again showed us his tongue, and rolled his eyes from one of us to the other, whoever we were.

Sister Anne produced a thermometer. With professional motions, which looked so much like showing off, and yet were so derogatory, she was shaking it down. "All right, Cousin Felix, that's enough for now! You pay attention to that sunset, and see what it's going to do! —Listen, that picture made twenty-six," she murmured. She was keeping some kind of tally in her head, as you do most exactly out of disbelief.

Uncle Felix held open his mouth and she popped the thermometer straight in, and he had to close it. It looked somehow wrong, dangerous—it was like daring to take the temperature of a bear.

"I don't know where he thinks he is," she said, nodding her head gently at him, Yes—yes.

Before I knew it, his hand raked my bare arm down. I felt as if I had been clawed, but when I bent toward him, the hand had fallen inert again on the bed, where it looked burnished with hundreds of country suns and today's on top of them all.

"Please, ma'am," said a treble voice at the door. A tow-headed child looked in solemnly; his little red tie shone as his hair did, as with dewdrops. "Miss Sister Anne, the man says it's one more and then you."

"Listen at that. My free picture," said Sister Anne, drawing breath like a little girl going to recite, about to be martyrized.

For whom! I thought.

"Don't you think I need to freshen up a little bit?" she said with a comical expression. "My hair hasn't been combed since four o'clock this morning."

"You go right ahead," said Kate. "Right ahead."

Sister Anne bent to sight straight into Uncle Felix's

face, and then took the thermometer out of his lips and sighted along it. She read off his temperature to herself and almost sweetly firmed her lips. That was *hers*, what he gave *her*.

Uncle Felix made a hoarse sound as she ran out again. Kate moved to the trunk, where on a stack of old books and plates was a water pitcher that did not look cold, and a spoon. She poured water into the spoon, and gave the old man some water on his tongue, which he offered her. But already his arm had begun to stir, to swing, and he put the same work-heavy, beast-heavy hand, all of a lump, against my side again and found my arm, which this time went loose in its socket, waiting. He groped and pulled at it, down to my hand. He pulled me all the way down. On my knees I found the pencil lying in the dust at my feet. He wanted it.

My Great-Uncle Felix, without his right hand ever letting me go, received the pencil in his left. For a moment our arms crossed, but it was not awkward or strange, more as though we two were going to skate off, or dance off, out of here. Still holding me, but without stopping a moment, as if all the thinking had already been done, he knocked open the old hymnbook on top of the mossy stack at the bedside and began riding the pencil along over the flyleaf; though none of the Jerrolds that I ever heard of were left-handed, and certainly not he. I turned away my eyes.

There, lying on the barrel in front of me, looking vaguely like a piece of worn harness, was an object which I slowly recognized as once beloved to me. It was a stereopticon. It belonged in the parlor, on the lower shelf of the round table in the middle of the room, with the Bible on the top. It belonged to Sunday and to summertime.

My held hand pained me through the wish to use it and

lift that old, beloved, once mysterious contraption to my
eyes, and dissolve my sight, all our sights, in that. In
that delaying, binding pain, I remembered Uncle Felix.
That is, I remembered the real Uncle Felix, and could
hear his voice, respectful again, asking the blessing at the
table. Then I heard the cataract of talk, which I knew
he engendered; that was what Sunday at Mingo began
with.

I remembered the house, the real house, always silvery,
as now, but then cypressy and sweet, cool, reflecting, dust-
less. Sunday dinner was eaten from the table pulled to
the very head of the breezeway, almost in the open door.
The Sunday air poured in through it, and through the
frail-ribbed fanlight and side lights, down on the island
we made, our cloth and our food and our flowers and
jelly and our selves, so lightly enclosed there—as though
we ate in pure running water. So many people were
gathered at Mingo that the Sunday table was pulled out
to the limit, from a circle to the shape of our race track.
It held my mother, my father and brother; Aunt Ethel;
Uncle Harlan, who could be persuaded, if he did not
eat too much, to take down the banjo later; my Jerrold
grandmother, who always spoke of herself as "nothing
but a country bride, darling," slicing the chicken while
Uncle Felix cut the ham; Cousin Eva and Cousin Archie;
and Kate, Kate everywhere, like me. And plenty more besides; it was eating against talking, all as if nobody would
ever be persuaded to get up and leave the table: everybody, we thought, that we needed. And some were so
pretty!

And when they were, the next thing, taking their naps
all over the house, it was then I got my chance, and there
would be, in lieu of any nap, pictures of the world to see.

I ran right through, with the stereopticon, straight **for** the front porch steps, and sitting there, stacked the slides between my bare knees in the spread of my starched skirt. The slide belonging on top was "The Ladies' View, Lakes of Killarney."

And at my side sat Uncle Felix.

That expectation—even alarm—that the awareness of happiness can bring! Of any happiness. It need not even be yours. It is like being able to prophesy, all of a sudden. Perhaps Uncle Felix loved the stereopticon most; he had it first. With his coat laid folded on the porch floor on the other side of him, sitting erect in his shirtsleeves for this, he would reach grandly for the instrument as I ran bringing it out. He saddled his full-size nose with the stereopticon and said, "All right, Skeeta." And then as he signaled ready for each slide, I handed it up to him.

Some places took him a long time. As he perspired there in his hard collar, looking, he gave off a smell like a cut watermelon. He handed each slide back without a word, and I was ready with the next. I would no more have spoken than I would have interrupted his blessing at the table.

Eventually they—all the rest of the Sunday children —were awake and wanting to be tossed about, and they hung over him, pulling on him, seeking his lap, his shoulders, pinning him down, riding on him. And he with his giant size and absorption went on looking his fill. It was as though, while he held the stereopticon to his eye, *we* did not see *him*. Gradually his ear went red. I thought all the blood had run up to his brain then, as it had run to mine.

It's strange to think that since then I've gone to live in one of those picture cities. If I asked him something about what was in there, he never told me more than a

name, never saw fit. (I couldn't read then.) We passed
each other those sand-pink cities and passionate foun-
tains, the waterfall that rocks snuffed out like a light,
islands in the sea, red Pyramids, sleeping towers, check-
ered pavements on which strollers had come out, with
shadows that seemed to steal further each time, as if the
strollers had moved, and where the statues had rainbow
edges; volcanoes; the Sphinx, and Constantinople; and
again the Lakes, like starry fields—brought forward each
time so close that it seemed to me the tracings from the
beautiful face of a strange coin were being laid against
my brain. Yet there were things too that I couldn't see,
which could make Uncle Felix pucker his lips as for a
kiss.

"Now! Dicey! I want *you* to tell me how I look!"

Sister Anne had opened the door, to a flash from the
front. A low growl filled the room.

"You look mighty dressed up," said Kate for me.

Sister Anne had put on a hat—a hat from no telling
where, what visit, what year, but it had been swashbuck-
ling. It was a sort of pirate hat—black, of course.

"Thank you. Oh! Everything comes at once if it comes
at all!" she said, looking piratically from one to the other
of us. "So you can't turn around fast enough! You come
on Mr. Dolollie's day! Now what will I do for Sunday!"

Under that, I heard an inching, delicate sound. Uncle
Felix had pulled loose the leaf of the book he had la-
bored over. Now he let me go, and took both swollen
fists and over the lump of his body properly folded his
page. He nudged it into my tingling hand.

"*He'll* keep you busy!" said Sister Anne nodding.
"*That* table looks ready to go to market!" Her eyes
were so bright, she was in such a state of excitement

and pride and suspense that she seemed to lose for the
moment all ties with us or the house or any remembrance
where anything was and what it was for. The next minute, with one blunder of her hatbrim against the door,
she s gone.

I had slipped the torn page from the book, still folded,
into my pocket, working it down through the starch-
stuck dimity. Now I leaned down and kissed Uncle Felix's long unshaven, unbathed cheek. He didn't look at
me—Kate stared, I felt it—but in a moment his eyes
pinched shut.

Kate turned her back and looked out the window. The
scent was burrowing into the roses, their heads hung.
Out there was the pasture. The small, velvety cows had
come up to the far fence and were standing there looking toward the house. They were little, low, black cows,
soot-black, with their calves among them, in a green that
seemed something to drink from more than something to
eat.

Kate groaned under her breath, "I don't care, I've
got to see her do it."

"She's doing it now," I said.

We stood on either side of the bed. Again Uncle Felix's head poked forward and held still, the western light
full and late on him now.

"Never mind, Uncle Felix. Listen to me, I'll be back,"
Kate said. "It's nothing—it's all nothing—"

I felt that I had just showed off a good deal in some
way. She bent down, hands on knees, but his face did
not consult either of us again, although his eyes had
opened. Tiptoeing modestly, we left him by himself. In
his bleached gown he looked like the story book picture
of the Big Bear, the old white one with star children on

his back and more star children following, in triangle dresses, starting down the Milky Way.

We saw Sister Anne at the table signing the book. We hid in the front bedroom before she saw us.

The overflow from outside was sitting in here. Thick around the room, on the rocking chair, on parlor chairs and the murmurous cane chairs from the dining room, our visitors were visiting. A few were standing or sitting at the windows to talk, and leaning against the mantle. The four-poster held, like a paddock, a collection of cleaned-up little children, mostly girls, some of them mutinous and tearful, one little girl patiently holding a fruit jar with something alive inside.

"Writing herself in, signing herself out all in one," Kate whispered, watching. "No! She mustn't forget that."

She gripped my wrist wickedly and we tiptoed out across the breezeway, and stood by the parlor curtain until Kate lifted it, and I saw her smile into the parlor to make watching all right; and perhaps I did the same.

Sister Anne was shaking out her skirt, and white crumbs scattered on the rug. She had managed a slice of that cake. The parlor in its plush was radiant in the spectacular glare of multiplied lights brought close around. The wallpaper of course was red, but now it had a cinnamon cast. Its design had gone into another one—it, too, faded and precise, ringed by rain and of a queerly intoxicating closeness, like an old trunk that has been opened still again for the children to find costumes. White flags and amaryllis in too big a vase, where they parted themselves in the middle and tried to fall out, were Sister Anne's idea of what completed the mantle shelf. The fireplace was banked with privet hedge, as for a country wedding. I could almost hear a wavery baritone voice singing, "O Promise Me."

One with his camera and flash apparatus, the photographer stood with his back to us. He was baldheaded. We could see over him; he was short, and he leaned from side to side. He had long since discarded his coat, and his suspenders crossed tiredly on that bent back.

Sister Anne sat one way, then the other. A variety of expressions traveled over her face—pensive, eager, wounded, sad, and businesslike.

"I don't know why she can't make up her mind," I said all at once. "She's done nothing but practice all afternoon."

"Wait, wait, wait," said Kate. "Let her get to it."

What would show in the picture was none of Mingo at all, but the itinerant backdrop—the same old thing, a scene that never was, a black and white and gray blur of unrolled, yanked-down moonlight, weighted at the bottom with the cast-iron parlor rabbit doorstop, just behind Sister Anne's restless heel. The photographer raised up with arms extended, as if to hold and balance Sister Anne just exactly as she was now, with some special kind of semaphore. But Sister Anne was not letting him off that easily.

"Just a minute—I feel like I've lost something!" she cried, in a voice of excitement. "My handkerchief?"

I could feel Kate whispering to me, sideways along my cheek.

"Did poor Uncle Felix have to kill somebody when he was young?"

"I don't know." I shrugged, to my own surprise.

"Do you suppose she told him today there was a Yankee in the house? He might be thinking of Yankees."
Kate slanted her whisper into my hair. It was more feel-

ing, than hearing, what she said. "But he was almost too young for killing them . . . Of course he wasn't too young to be a drummer boy . . ." Her words sighed away.

I shrugged again.

"Mama can tell us! I'll make her tell us. What did the note say, did it go on just warning us to hide?"

I shook my head. But she knew I must have looked at it.

"Tell you when we get out," I whispered back, stepping forward a little from her and moving the curtain better.

"Oh, wait!" Sister Anne exclaimed again.

I could never have cared, or minded, less how Sister Anne looked. I had thought of what was behind the photographer's backdrop. It was the portrait in the house, the one picture on the walls of Mingo, where pictures ordinarily would be considered frivolous. It hung just there on the wall that was before me, crowded between the windows, high up—the romantic figure of a young lady seated on a fallen tree under brooding skies: my Great-Grandmother Jerrold, who had been Evelina Mackaill.

And I remembered—rather, more warmly, *knew*, like a secret of the family—that the head of this black-haired, black-eyed lady who always looked the right, mysterious age to be my sister, had been fitted to the ready-made portrait by the painter who had called at the door—he had taken the family off guard, I was sure of it, and spoken to their pride. The yellow skirt spread fanlike, straw hat held ribbon-in-hand, orange beads big as peach pits (to conceal the joining at the neck)—none of that, any more than the forest scene so unlike the Mississippi wilderness (that enormity she had been carried to as a bride, when the logs of this house were cut, her bounded world by drop by drop of sweat exposed, where she'd died in the end of yellow fever) or the melancholy clouds obscuring the sky behind the passive figure with the small, crossed feet—none of it, world or body, was really hers. *She* had eaten bear meat, seen Indians, she had married into the wilderness at Mingo, to what unknown feelings. Slaves had died in her arms. She had grown a rose for Aunt Ethel to send back by me. And still those eyes, opaque, all pupil, belonged to Evelina—I knew, because they saw out, as mine did; weren't warned, as mine weren't, and never shut before the end, as mine would not. I, her divided sister, knew who had felt the wildness of the world behind the ladies' view. We were homesick for somewhere that was the same place.

I returned the touch of Kate's hand. This time, I whispered, "What he wrote was, 'River—Daisy—Midnight—Please.' "

" 'Midnight'!" Kate cried first. Then, "River daisy? His mind has wandered, the poor old man."

"Daisy's a lady's name," I whispered impatiently, so impatiently that the idea of the meeting swelled right out of the moment, and I even saw Daisy.

Then Kate whispered, "You must mean Beck, Dicey, that was his wife, and he meant her to meet him in Heaven. Look again.—*Look* at Sister Anne!"

Sister Anne had popped up from the organ bench. Whirling around, she flung up the lid—hymnbooks used to be stuffed inside—and pulled something out. To our amazement and delight, she rattled open a little fan, somebody's old one—it even sounded rusty. As she sat down again she drew that fan, black and covered over with a shower of forget-me-nots, languidly across her bosom. The photographer wasted not another moment. The flash ran wild through the house, singeing our very hair at the door, filling our lungs with gunpowder smoke as though there had been a massacre. I had a little fit of coughing.

"Now let her try forgiving herself for this," said Kate, and almost lazily folded her arms there.

"Did you see me?" cried Sister Anne, running out crookedly and catching onto both of us to stop herself. "Oh, I hope it's good! Just as the thing went off—I blinked!" She laughed, but I believed I saw tears start out of her eyes. "Look! Come meet Mr. Puryear. Come have your pictures taken! It's only a dollar down and you get them in the *mail!*"

And for a moment, I wanted to—wanted to have my picture taken, to be sent in the mail to someone—even against that absurd backdrop, having a vain, delicious wish to torment someone, then have something to laugh about together afterwards.

Kate drew on ladylike white cotton gloves, that I had not noticed her bringing. Whatever she had been going to say turned into, "Sister Anne? What have you been telling Uncle Felix?"

"What I *didn't* tell him," replied Sister Anne, "was that people were getting their pictures taken: I didn't want him to feel left out. It was just for one day. Mr. Alf J. Puryear is the photographer's name—there's some Puryears in Mississippi. I'll always remember his sad face."

"Thank you for letting us see Uncle Felix, in spite of the trouble we were," said Kate in her clear voice.

"You're welcome. And come back. But if I know the signs," said Sister Anne, and looked to me, the long-lost, for confirmation of herself the specialist, "we're losing him fast, ah me. Well! I'm used to it, I can stand it, that's what I'm for. But oh, I can't stand for you all to go!

Stay—stay!" And she turned into our faces that outrageous, yearning smile she had produced for the photographer.

I knew I hadn't helped Kate out yet about Sister Anne. And so I said, "Aunt Ethel didn't come today! Do you know why? Because she just can't abide you!"

The bright lights inside were just then turned off. Kate and I turned and ran down the steps, just as a voice out of the porch shadow said, "It seems to me that things are moving in too great a rush." It sounded sexless and ageless both to me; it sounded deaf.

Somehow, Kate and I must have expected everybody to rush out after us. Sister Anne's picture, the free one, had been the last. But nobody seemed to be leaving. Children were the only ones flying loose. Maddened by the hour and the scene, they were running barefoot and almost silent, skimming around and around the house. The others sat and visited on, in those clouds of dust, all holding those little tickets or receipts I remembered wilting in their hands; some of the old men had them stuck in their winter hats. At last, maybe the Lady Baltimore cake would have to be passed.

"Sister Anne, greedy and all as she is, will cut that cake yet, if she can keep them there a little longer!" said Kate in answer to my thoughts.

"Yes," I said.

"She'll forget what you said. Oh the sweet evening air!"

I took so for granted once, and when had I left for ever, I wondered at that moment, the old soft airs of Mingo as I knew them—the interior airs that were always kitchen-like, of oil lamps, wood ashes, and that golden scrapement off cake-papers—and outside, beyond the just-watered ferns lining the broad strong railing,

the fragrances winding up through the luster of the fields
and the dim, gold screen of trees and the river beyond,
fragrances so rich I once could almost see them, untrans-
parent and Oriental? In those days, fresh as I was from
Sunday School in town, I could imagine the Magi riding
through, laden.

At other times—perhaps later, during visits back from
the North—that whole big congregated outside smell,
like the ripple of an animal's shining skin, used suddenly
to travel across and over to my figure standing on the
porch, like a marvel of lightning, and by it I could see
myself, by myself, a child on a visit to Mingo, hardly
under any auspices that I knew of, but wild myself, at
the mercy of that touch.

"It's a wonder she didn't let the niggers file in at the
back and have theirs taken too. If you didn't know it was
Sister Anne, it would be past understanding," Kate said.
"It would kill Mama—we must spare her this."

"Of course!" Sparing was our family trait.

We were going down the walk, measuredly, like lady
callers who had left their cards; in single file. That was
the one little strip of cement in miles and miles—narrow
as a ladder.

"But listen, who was Daisy, have you thought? *Daisy*,"
said Kate in front. She looked over her shoulder. "I don't
believe it."

I smoothed out that brown page of the hymn book with
the torn edge, that purple indelible writing across it
where the print read "Round & Shaped Notes." Coming
around, walking in the dampening uncut grass, I showed
it to Kate. You could still make out the big bold **D** with
the cap on.

" '*Midnight!*' But they always go to bed at dark, out
here."

I put the letter back inside my pocket. Kate said, "Daisy must have been smart. I don't understand that message at all."

"Oh, I do," I lied. I felt it was up to me. I told Kate, "It's a kind of shorthand." Yet it had seemed a very long letter—didn't it take Uncle Felix a long time to write it!

"Oh, I can't think even out here, but mustn't Daisy be dead? . . . Not Beck?" Kate ventured, then was wordless.

"Daisy was Daisy," I said. It was the "please" that had hurt me. It was I who put the old iron ring over the gate and fastened it. I saw the Cape Jessamines were all in bud, and for a moment, just at the thought, I seemed to reel from a world too fragrant, just as I suspected Aunt Ethel had reeled from one too loud.

"I expect by now Uncle Felix has got his names mixed up, and Daisy was a mistake," Kate said.

She could always make the kind of literal remark, like this, that could alienate me, even when we were children —much as I love her. I don't know why, yet, but some things are too important for a mistake even to be considered. I was sorry I had showed Kate the message, and said, "Look, how we've left him by himself."

We stood looking back, in our wonder, until out of the house came the photographer himself, all packed up—a small, hurrying man, black-coated as his subjects were. He wore a pale straw summer hat, which was more than they had. It was to see him off, tell him good-by, reassure him, that they had waited.

"Open it again! Look out, Dicey," said Kate, "get back."

He did not tarry. With paraphernalia to spare, he ran out between the big bushes ahead of us with a strange,

rushing, fuse-like, Yankee sound—out through the evening and into his Ford, and was gone like that.

I felt the secret pang behind him—I know I did feel
the cheat he had found and left in the house, the helpless, asking cheat. I felt it more and more, too strongly.

And then we were both excruciated by our terrible
desire, and catching each other at the same moment with
almost fierce hands, we did it, we laughed. We leaned
against each other and on the weak, open gate, and
gasped and choked into our handkerchiefs, and finally
we cried. "Maybe she kissed him!" cried Kate at random.
Each time we tried to stop ourselves, we sought each
other's faces and started again. We laughed as though
we were inspired.

"She forgot to take the pencil out of her hair!" gasped
Kate.

"Oh no! What do you think Uncle Felix wrote with!
He managed—it was the pencil out of Sister Anne's
head!" That was almost too much for me. I held onto
the gate.

I was aware somehow that birds kept singing passionately all around us just the same, and hurling themselves
like bolts in front of our streaming eyes.

Kate tried to say something new—to stop us disgrac-
ing ourselves and each other, our visit, our impending
tragedy, Aunt Ethel, everything. Not that anybody, anything in the world could hear us, reeled back in those
bushes now, except ourselves.

"You know Aunt Beck—she never let us leave Mingo
without picking us our nosegay on the way down this
walk, every little thing she grew that smelled nice, pinks,
four-o'clocks, verbena, heliotrope, bits of nicotiana—she
grew all such little things, just for that, Di. And she
wound their stems, round and round and round, with a

black or white thread she would take from a needle in her collar, and set it all inside a rose-geranium leaf, and presented it to you at the gate—right here. That was Aunt Beck," said Kate's positive voice. "She wouldn't *let* you leave without it."

But it was no good. We had not laughed together that way since we were too little to know any better.

With tears streaming down my cheeks, I said, "I don't remember her."

"But she wouldn't *let* you forget. She *made* you remember her!"

Then we stopped.

I stood there and folded the note back up. There was the house, floating on the swimming dust of evening, its gathered, safe-shaped mass darkening. A dove in the woods called its five notes—two and three—at first unanswered. The last gleam of sunset, except for the threadbare curtain of wistaria, could be seen going on behind. The cows were lowing. The dust was in windings, the roads in their own shapes in the air, the exhalations of where the people all had come from.

"They'll all be leaving now," said Kate. "It's first-dark, almost."

But the grouping on the porch still held, that last we looked back, posed there along the rail, quiet and obscure and never-known as passengers on a ship already embarked to sea. Their country faces were drawing in even more alike in the dusk, I thought. Their faces were like dark boxes of secrets and desires to me, but locked safely, like old-fashioned caskets for the safe conduct of jewels on a voyage.

Something moved. The little girl came out to the front, holding her glass jar, like a dark lantern, outwards. Kate and I turned, wound our arms around each other, and got down to the car. We heard the horses.

It was all one substance now, one breath and density of blue. Along the back where the pasture was, the little, low black cows came in, in a line toward the house, with their sober sides one following the other. Where each went looked like simply where nothing was. But across the quiet we heard Theodore talking to them.

Across the road was Uncle Theodore's cabin, where clumps of privet hedge in front were shaped into a set of porch furniture, god-size, table and chairs, and a snake was hung up in a tree.

We drew out of the line of vehicles, and turned back down the dark blue country road. We neither talked, confided, nor sang. Only once, in a practical voice, Kate spoke.

"I hate going out there without Mama. Mama's too nice to say it about Sister Anne, but I will. You know what it is: it's in there somewhere."

Our lips moved together. "She's common . . ."

All around, something went on and on. It was hard without thinking to tell whether it was a throbbing, a dance, a rattle, or a ringing—all louder as we neared the bridge. It was everything in the grass and trees. Presently Mingo church, where Uncle Felix had been turned down on "knick-knack," revolved slowly by, with its faint churchyard. Then all was April night. I thought of my sweetheart, riding, and wondered if he were writing to me.

Going to Naples

The *Pomona* sailing out of New York was bound for Palermo and Naples. It was the warm September of a Holy Year. Along with the pilgrims and the old people going home, there rode in *turistica* half a dozen pairs of mothers and daughters—these seemed to take up the most room. If Mrs. C. Serto, going to Naples, might miss by a hair's breadth being the largest mother, there was no question about which was the largest daughter—that was hers. And how the daughter did love to scream! From the time the *Pomona* began to throb and move down the river, Gabriella Serto regaled the deck with clear, soprano cries. As she romped up and down after the other girls—she was the youngest, too: eighteen—screaming and waving good-by to the Statue of Liberty, a hole broke through her stocking and her flesh came through like a pear.

Before land was out of sight, everybody knew that whatever happened during the next two weeks at sea, Gabriella had a scream in store for it. It was almost as though their ship—not a large ship at all, the rumor began to go round—had been appointed for this. "Why do I have to be taken to Naples! Why? I was happy in Buffalo, with you and Papa and Aunt Rosalia and Uncle Enrico!" she wailed to her mother along the passages—

where of course everybody else, as well as the Sertos, was lost.

"Enough for you it is *l'Anno Santo*," said Mama. "Hold straight those shoulders. Look the others."

The others were going to pair off any minute—as far as pairing would go. There were six young girls, but though there were six young men too, they were only Joe Monteoliveto, Aldo Scampo, Poldy somebody, and three for the priesthood. As for Poldy, he was a Polish-American who was on his way now to marry a girl in Italy that he had never seen.

Every morning, to reach their deck, Mrs. Serto and Gabriella had to find their way along the whole length of the ship, right along its humming and pounding bottom, where the passage was wet (Did the ship leak? people asked) and narrow as a schoolroom aisle; past the quarters of the crew—who looked wild in their half-undress, even their faces covered with black—and the *Pomona* engines; and at last up a steep staircase toward the light. Gabriella complained all the way. Mrs. Serto, feeling this was the uphill journey, only puffed. On the long way back to the dining room—downhill—Mrs. Serto had her say.

"You saw! Every girl on ship is fat"—exactly what she said about school and church at home. "In *Napoli*, when I was a girl, your *Nonna* told me a hundred times, 'Little daughter: girls do well to be strong. Also, be *delicata*.' You wait! She'll tell you the same. What's the matter? You got pretty little feet like me." Mama framed herself in the engine-room door, and showed her shoe.

But not every girl coming into the dining room had to pass seven tables to reach her own, as Gabriella did—bouncing along sideways, with each table to measure her hips again as briskly as a mother's tape measure; while

Joe Monteoliveto, for example, might be looking her way.

"You are youngest of six daughters, all beautiful and strong, five married to smart boys, Maria's Arrigo smart enough to be pharmacist. Five with babies to show. And what would you call every one those babies?"

The word rushed out. "Adorable!"

"*Bellissimo!* But you hang back."

"So O.K.! If you wouldn't follow me all the time!"

"I know the time to drop behind," said Mama sharply.

On deck all day, where she could see all that water, the smoother the ocean looked behind, the more apprehensive Gabriella felt; tourist deck faced backwards. She yelled that she wished the ship would turn around right where it was and take her back to the good old Statue of Liberty again. At that, Mama cast her eyes heavenward and a little to the left, like St. Cecilia on the cake plate at home, won on stunt night at the Sodality.

"Walk!" said the mothers to their daughters.

"You hear, Gabriella? Get up and walk!"

There was nowhere to go but in a circle—six of them walking arm-in-arm, dissolved in laughter; Maria-Pia Arpista almost had to be held up—especially when they wheeled at the turns and Gabriella gave her scream. For every time, there were the same black shawls, the same old caps, backed up against the blue—faces coming out of them that grew to be the only faces in the world, more solid a group than a family's, more persistent one by one than faces held fast in the memory or floating to nearness in dreams. On the best benches sat the old people, old enough to be going home to die—not noticing of the water, of the bad smells here and there, of where the warnings read "*Pittura Fresca*," or when the loudspeaker cried "*Attenzione!*" and the others flew to the rail to learn the worst. They cared only for which side of the boat the sun was shining on. If they heard Gabriella screaming, it would be hard to tell. They could not even speak English.

On the last bench on one side two black men sat together by themselves. They never said a word, they did not smile. Their feet were long as loaves of bread, and black as beetles, and each pair pointed outward east and west; together their four feet formed a big black M, for getting married, set out for young girls to fall over.

"Why you put your tongue out those black people? Is that nice?" said Mama. "Signora Arpista, your Maria-Pia needs to sit down, look her expression."

But by the third day out, Maria-Pia walked with Joe Monteoliveto, and her expression had changed. So did Mama's—she stepped up and joined Maria-Pia's mama, a few paces behind the new couple's heels, where she would get in on everything.

Gabriella took a long running jump to the other side of the deck. And there, only a little distance away, stood Aldo Scampo, all by himself, as though the breezes had just set him down. He stood at the rail looking out, his rich pompadour blowing. The shadow of the upper deck hung over him like a big jaw, or the lid of a trunk, with priests on it.

As Gabriella drew near, slowly, as though she brought bad news, he leaned low on his elbows, watching the birds drop into the water where the crew, below, were shooting guns through the portholes. Except for white frown marks, Aldo's forehead was all bright copper, and so were his nose and chin, his chest, his folded arms—as if he were dressed up in somebody's kitchen dowry over his well-known costume of yellow T-shirt and old army pants. The story Mama had of Aldo Scampo was that he was unmarried, was *Californese,* had mother, father, sisters, and brothers in America, and his mother's people lived in Nettuno, where they partly owned a boat; but as he rattled around in a cabin to himself, the complete story was not yet known.

Pop—pop—pop.

These were the small, tireless, black-and-gold island birds that had kept up with their ship so far today that Gabriella felt like telling them, "Go home, dopes"—only of course, having followed for such a long way, by now they could never fly all the way back. ("*Attenzione!*" the loudspeaker had warned—all for some land you couldn't see, the Azores.) Another small body plummeted down before Aldo, so close he might have caught it in his hand. Did Aldo Scampo, mopping his radiant brow, know how many poor little birds that made?

Like a mind-reader, he turned brilliantly toward her; she thought he was going to answer with the number of birds, but when he spoke it was even more electrifying than an answer; it was a question.

"Ping pong?"

She screamed and raced him to the table.

This must have been the very moment that Aldo Scampo himself gave something up. Until now he had not had more than a passing glance for the girls who went walking by in a row with their chocolate cigarettes in the air. Like Joe Monteoliveto before him, he had brooded over La Zìngara, the popular passenger said to be an actress; there she was now, further down the rail, talking to an almost *old* man. As Aldo and Gabriella pounded past her, La Zìngara—thin, but no one could say how young—leaned back into a life preserver as though it were a swing.

Her lips, moving like a scissors, could be read: she was talking about the Jersey Highway.

While Aldo went begging the balls from the children, Gabriella seized her paddle and beat the table like an Indian drum. In a moment, many drew near.

Up to now, Gabriella's only partner had been a choice between a boy of nine, who had since broken his arm and would have to wear a sling to see the Pope, and the Polish-American fellow, who was engaged. Both, of course, had beaten her—but not as she would be beaten today! And her extra-long skirt, made by Mama in a nice strong red for the trip, rocked on her like a panoply as she readied herself for the opening ball, and missed it.

Everybody cheered. Even if she did not miss the ball, Gabriella was almost certain to fall down; finally, rushing in an ill-advised arc, she did collide with a priest, a large one, who was down from above to see how things in *turistica* were going. He rolled away in his skirts like a ball of yarn and had to be picked up by two of the three for the priesthood, while Gabriella clapped her hands to her ears and yelped like a puppy.

Everybody had begun to wonder if Gabriella could help screaming—especially now, after three days. It was true her screams were sometimes justified, out on a ship at sea, and always opportune—but there were also screams that seemed offered through the day for their own sake, endeavors of pure anguish or joy that youth and strength seemed able to put out faster than the steady, pounding quiet of the voyage could ever overtake and heal.

Only her long brows were calm in her face with its widened mouth, stretched eyes, and flying dark hair, in her whole contending body, as though some captive, that had never had news of the world, land or sea, would some-

times stand there and look out from that pure arch—but
never to speak; that could not even be thought to hear.

The evening after her overthrow at ping pong, the
dining room saw Gabriella come to the door and for a
breath pause there. There was an ineffable quality about
Mrs. Serto's daughter now. An evening after a storm
comes with such bright drops—so does a child whose tan-
trum is over, even the reason for it almost, if not quite,
forgotten. Through large, oval eyes whose shine made
them look over-forgiving, she regarded the dining room
now. And as she came through the door, they saw appearing from behind her Aldo Scampo, almost luminous himself in a clean white shirt.

As she and Aldo started hand in hand across the
room, there was a sudden *"Tweeeeet!"* Papa, an old man
from the table farthest back in the corner, blew a tin
whistle whenever he felt like it—his joke and his privilege.
Immediately everybody laughed.

Was it on every boat that tried to cross the ocean
that some old fellow and his ten-cent whistle alerted the
whole assembly at life's most precious moments? Papa
was an outrageous, halfway dirty, twice-married old man
in an olive-green sweater who at each meal fought for
the whole carafe of wine for himself and then sent the
waiter for another. On top of his long head rose a crest
of grizzly hair. A fatherly mustache, well-stained,
draped itself over the whistle when he blew it. Except
for one old crippled lady in this room, he was surely the
only Italian in the world who could cross the ocean without suffering for it at all. His black eyes were forever
traveling carelessly beyond his own table. And just
when it was least expected, when it was least desired,
when your thoughts were all gentle and reassured and

forgiving and triumphant—then it would be your turn:
"Tweeeeet!"

Gabriella and Aldo, after stopping dead in their
tracks—for there was something official about the sound
—marched to their separate tables like punished children. But by the time Gabriella had reached hers safely,
she was able to lift her face like a dish of something
fresh and delicious she had brought straight to them;
and Mrs. Serto smiled her circle round: Mr. Fossetta,
for Bari; Poldy, who was engaged, and Mr. Ambrogio,
for Rome.

"Dressed up!" said Mama, a gesture of blessing for
all falling from her plump little hand. Mama was even
more dressed up. They had on silk blouses.

"We've been strolling, with Maria-Pia and Joe!" And
Gabriella took her seat on Mama's right hand.

Tonight, the dining room felt, the missing sixth
should have been at that table. Between Poldy and Mr.
Ambrogio waited the vacant chair and spotless napkin
of one assigned who had never come. Even if appetite
had gone, he should have shown his face to complete the
happiness of a mother.

Later that very night, Gabriella was fallen against
Mrs. Serto on the rearmost bench on deck, trying not
to watch the flagpole ride, while at gentle intervals her
mother gave her a little more of the account of the bride's
dress reported to be traveling on this ship in the Polish-
American's cabin. Without those screams, the *Pomona*
sailed in a strange, almost sad tranquillity under the
stars, as in a trance that might never be broken again.
So there had come a night, almost earlier than they had
expected, when they all had their chance to feel sorry
for Gabriella.

Between tea and dinner time next day, everybody who was able was sitting about on the benches enjoying the warm sea. All afternoon, with the sun going down on their backs, they had been drawing nearer and nearer the tinted coast of Spain. It grew long, pink, and caverned as the side of a melon. Chances were it would never come close enough for them to see much: they would see no face. But to Gabriella, the faces here on deck appeared bemused enough. Beside her, sitting up on their bench, Mama seemed to be asleep, with Mrs. Arpista, beyond her, also asleep; the two maternal heads under their little black buns nodded together like twin buoys in the waves.

Only the two black men looked the same as always. Not yet had they laughed, or asked a single question. Not yet had they expressed consternation at mealtime, or a moment's doubt about the course of the ship. Their very faith was enough to put other passengers off.

Aldo Scampo, like a man pining to be teased, was reading. He lay sprawled in the solitary deck chair— the one that the steward had opened out and set up in the center of the deck to face everybody, and labeled "Crosby"—very likely the name of the unattached lady who could not speak a word of Italian. All afternoon Aldo had held at various angles in front of his eyes a paper-back book bought on board, *The Bandit Giuliano, Dopo Bellolampo*. Or else he got up and disappeared into the public room to drink cherry soda and play cards with three little gray fellows going to Foggia.

When Aldo was about to open that book again, Gabriella rose from Mama's bench, took a hop, skip and jump to the chair, and pulled Aldo out of it. He came down to the deck floor on hands and knees, with a laughable crash.

She dropped beside him to make a violent face into his. Aldo, as though he drew a gun from a holster, put up a toothpick between his lips. On the softly vibrating floor, ringed around with the well-filled benches, they knelt confronting each other, eyes open wide. Just out of range, the ship's cat picked his way in and out the circle of feet, then, cradled in a pair of horny hands, disappeared upward.

It did not matter that the passengers on the warm *Pomona* deck had heads that were nodding or dreaming of home. It took only their legs from the knees down to listen like ears and watch like eyes—to wait dense and still as a ring of trees come near. The sailors softly beating the air with their paintbrushes, up in Second Class, could look down and see them too, over the signs *"Pittura Fresca"* hung on ropes festooning the stairs.

Aldo's and Gabriella's hands suddenly interlocked, and their arms were as immobilized as wings that failed. Gabriella drove her face into Aldo's warm shirt. She set her teeth into his sleeve. But when she pierced that sleeve she found his arm—rigid and wary, with a muscle that throbbed like a heart. She would have bitten a piece out of him then and there for the scare his arm gave her, but he moved like a spring and struck at her with his playful weapon, the toothpick between his teeth. In return she butted his chest, driving her head against the hard, hot rayon, while, still in the character of an airy bird, he pecked with his little beak that place on the back of the neck where women no longer feel. (Weren't all women made alike? she wondered: *she* could no longer feel there.) She screamed as if she could feel everything. But if she hadn't screamed so hard at Aldo yesterday, she wouldn't have had to bite him today. Now she knew *that* about Aldo.

The circle was still. Mama's own little feet might speak to them—there they rested, so well known. For a space Mama opened her eyes and contemplated her screaming daughter as she would the sunset behind her.

"Help! He's killing me!" howled Gabriella, but Mama dropped her eyes and was nodding Mrs. Arpista's way again.

Aldo buried his face in Gabriella's blouse, and she looked out over his head and presently smiled—not into any face in particular. Her smile was as rare as her silence, and as vulnerable—it was meant for everybody. A gap where a tooth was gone showed childishly.

And it lifted the soul—for a thing like crossing the ocean could depress it—to sit in the sun and contemplate among companions the weakness and the mystery of the flesh. Looking, dreaming, down at Gabriella, they felt something of an old, pure loneliness come back to them —like a bird sent out over the waters long ago, when they were young, perhaps from their same company. Only the long of memory, the brave and experienced of heart, could bear such a stirring, an awakening—first to have listened to that screaming, and in a flash to remember what it was.

Aldo climbed to his feet and set himself back in his chair, and Gabriella went back to her mother, but the *Pomona*, turning, sailed on to the south, down the coast of Europe—so near now that Father's vesper bell might almost be taken for a little goat bell on shore. The air colored, and a lighthouse put up its arm.

Even the morning sky told them they were in the Mediterranean now. They could see it glowing through the windows of church, while waiting for Father to come and start Mass. In the middle of the night before, they had slipped through the Gates of Gibraltar—even touched there, so it was said. While everybody was asleep, the two black passengers had been put off the boat.

"They're going to the Cape Verde Islands," Mrs. Arpista cried to Mrs. Serto two rows ahead. "They don't know nothing but French."

"*Poveretti!*" Mrs. Serto cried back, with the sympathy that comes too late. "And where were their wives, *i Mori?*"

"My sweetheart and I are going to have a happy, happy Christmas," Poldy announced, rubbing his hands together. His straw-blond hair was thin enough to show a baby-like scalp beneath.

"So you never seen your girl, eh?" remarked Mr. Fossetta, a small dark father of five, who sat just in front of him. All the Serto table sat together in church—Mama thought it was nice. Today they made a little square around her. At her right, Poldy locked his teeth and gave a dazzling grin.

"We've never seen each other. But do we love each other? Oh boy!"

Mr. Fossetta made the abrupt gesture with which he turned away the fresh sardines at the table, and faced front again.

Poldy reached in his breast pocket and produced his papers. He prodded under the elastic band that held them all together to take out a snapshot, and passed this up to Mr. Fossetta. The first time he'd tried to pass that was in the middle of the movie while the lights blinked on for them to change the reel.

"Yes, a happy, happy Christmas," said Poldy. "Pass that. Why *wouldn't* we be happy, we'll be married then. I'm taking the bridesmaids' dresses, besides the bride's I told you about, and her mother's dress too, in store boxes. Her aunt in Chicago, that's who gave me the address in the first place—she knows everything! The names and the sizes. Everything is going to fit. Wait! I'll show you something else—the ticket I bought for my wife to come back to the U.S.A. on. Guess who we're going to live with? Her aunt."

Everybody took a chance to yawn or look out the window, but Mama inclined her head at Poldy going through his papers and said, "Sweetest thing in the world, Christmas, second to love." She suddenly looked to the other side of her. "You paying attention, Gabriella?"

Gabriella had been examining her bruises, old and new. She shook her head; under the kerchief it was burgeoning with curlers. Here came the snapshot on its way from the row ahead.

"Take that bride," said Mama.

"Hey, she's little!" said Gabriella. "You can't hardly see her."

Old Papa put his head in the door, gave Gabriella his red eye, and vanished. He was only passing by, the ship's cat in his arms, with no intention in the world of coming in, but he looked in.

Poldy reached across Mama as though she were nothing but a man. That golden-haired wrist with its yellow-gold watch was under Gabriella's nose, and those golden-haired fingers snatched the picture from her and Mama's hands and stuck it at Mr. Ambrogio, behind.

"Wait, wait! There went who I love best in world," said Mama. "Little bride. Was that nice?"

"We haven't got all day," said Poldy. "Gee, I can't

find her ticket anywhere. Don't worry, folks, I'll show
it to you at breakfast."

"She knows how to pose," said Mr. Ambrogio politely.
He was a widower of long standing.

"All right, pass it."

At that moment, who but Aldo Scampo elected to come
to church! Just in time, as he dropped to his knee by
the last chair in the row, to be greeted with Poldy's bride
stuck under his nose.

"Curlers!" hissed Mama in Gabriella's ear. She gave
Gabriella's cheek one of her incredibly quick little slaps
—it looked for all the world like only a pat, belonging
to no time and place but pure motherhood.

There Aldo studied the bride from his knees, sighting
down his blue chin before breakfast.

"O.K., O.K., partner!" said Poldy, his hand on the
reach again, as Father came bustling in with fresh paint
on his skirts; and there was quiet except for two noisy,
almost simultaneous smacks: Poldy kissing his bride and
snapping her back under the elastic band.

"You stay after Mass and confess sloth, you hear?"
whispered Mama.

Gabriella and Aldo were looking along the rows of
rolled-down eyelids at each other. They put out exactly
simultaneous tongues.

By nine o'clock, Gabriella and Aldo were strolling up
on deck; so was everybody. Aldo pushed out his lips
and offered Gabriella a kiss.

"Oh, look what I found," said Mrs. Serto from behind them, causing them to jump apart as if she'd exploded something. She had opened a little gold locket.
Now she held out, cupped in her pink palm, a ragged

little photograph, oval and pearl-colored, snatched from its frame. "Who but my Gabriella as a baby?"

Gabriella seized it, where Mama bent over it smiling as at a little foundling, and tucked it inside her blouse.

"No longer a child now, Gabriella," announced Mama to the sky.

"Somebody told me," Aldo said, "it's nifty up front."

"*Cielo azzurro!*" said Mama. "Go 'head. *Pellegrini, pellegrini* everywhere, beautiful day like this!"

Three priests strolled by, their skirts gaily blowing, and as Joe Monteoliveto ran their gamut, juggling ping pong balls, Mama held Gabriella fast for a moment and whispered, "Not the prize Arpistas may think—he leaves the boat at Palermo."

"Keep my purse," was all Gabriella said.

The long passage through the depths of the ship, that was too narrow for Mrs. Serto and Gabriella to walk without colliding, seemed made for Gabriella and Aldo. True, it was close with the smell of the sour wine the crew drank. In the deepest part, the engines pounding just within that open door made a human being seem to go in momentary danger of being shaken asunder. It sounded here a little like the Niagara Falls at home, but she had never paid much attention to *them.* Yet with all the deafening, Gabriella felt as if she and Aldo were walking side by side in some still, lonely, even high place never seen before now, with mountains above, valleys below, and sky. The old man in the red knit cap who slept all day on top of that box was asleep where he always was, but now as if he floated, with no box underneath him at all, in some spell. Even the grandfather clock, even the map, when these came into sight, looked faceless, part of a landscape. And the remembered sign, so beautifully penned, on the bulletin board—"Lost, a golden brooch for the tie, with initials F. A."—it shone at them like a star.

By steep stairs at the end, they came out on an altogether new deck, where the air was bright and stiff as an open eye. It was white and narrowing, set about with mysterious shapes of iron wound with chains. No passenger was in sight. Leaning into the very beak ahead, with her back to them, a *cameriera* was drying her hair; when she let it loose from the towel it blew behind her straight as an arm. A sailor, seated cross-legged on an eminence like a drum, with one foot bare, the blackened toes fanned out like a circus clown's, sewed with all his might on a sock with a full shape to it. All was still. No —as close as a voice that was speaking to them now, the *Pomona* was parting the water.

"Wait—a—minute," said Aldo still looking, with his hands on his hips.

So this was where Miss Crosby came with her book. Still as a mouse, she was sitting on the floor close to the rail, drawn up with the book on her knees.

"Don't bother her, and maybe she won't bother us," said Gabriella. "That's how *I* treat people."

Aldo came back, reached in his hand, and took the picture away from Gabriella, then sat down cross-legged on this barely slanting floor to see what he'd got.

At last he hit his leg a slap. He said, "They took one of me the same age! They had me dressed up like a little St. John the Baptist. Can you beat 'em?"

Gabriella had been standing behind him, where she could see anew. Suddenly she grasped a length of the hem of her skirt and blindfolded him with it. Aldo threw up both hands, the hand with the snapshot releasing it to the milky sea. The uncovered part of his face expressed solemnity. Like all blindfolded persons, he was holding his breath. Gabriella couldn't see his face; hers above it waited with eyes tight-shut.

A moment went by, and she jumped away; that was all that had come to her to do. Aldo promptly wheeled himself around, one leg flailing the deck, and caught her by the ankle and threw her.

She came down headlong; her fall, like a single clap of thunder, was followed by that burst of expectancy in the air that can almost be heard too. The *cameriera* bound down her hair, and the sailor put on his sock; as if they'd been together a long time, they disappeared together through the door, down the stairs.

Neither Gabriella nor Aldo stirred. They lay, a little apart, like the victims of a passing wind. Presently Aldo, moving one finger at a time, began to thump on the calf of Gabriella's leg—1, 2, 3, 4—while she lay as before, with her back to him. Intermittently the 1, 2, 3, 4 kept up, then it slowed and fell away. Gradually the sounds of the dividing sea came back to Gabriella's ear, as though a seashell were once more held lifted.

She turned her head and opened her eyes onto Aldo's clay-colored shoe, hung loose on his sockless foot. Far away now was his hand, gaping cavelike in sleep beside her forgotten leg. Past the pink buttress of his jaw rose the little fountain, not playing now, where his mouth stood open to the sky. He lay there sound asleep over the Mediterranean Sea.

Gabriella stayed as she was, caught in an element as languorous as it was strange, like a mermaid who has been netted into a fisherman's boat, only to find that the fisherman is dreaming. Where no eye oversaw them, the sea lifted and dropped them both, mindless as a cradle, up and down.

Even when La Zìngara clattered out on deck, with a
spectacled youth at her heels, and, seeing Aldo, gave the
sharp laugh of experience, Aldo only shut his lips, like
a reader who has just licked his finger to turn a page.
But Gabriella sat up and caught her hair and her skirt,
seeing those horn-rims: that young man was marked for
the priesthood.

With the pop of corks being drawn from wine bot-
tles, La Zìngara kicked off her shoes. Then she began
dancing in her polished, bare feet over the deck. ("Prac-
ticing," she had replied with her knifelike smile when
the mothers wondered where she went all day—furiously
watching an actress rob the church.) She made the horn-
rimmed young man be her partner; to dance like La Zìngara meant having someone to catch you. In a few turns
they had bounded to the other side of the deck.

"Excuse me," said a new voice. Miss Crosby had unfolded herself and come over on her long legs. Speaking
across the sleeping Aldo as though she only called through
a window, she asked, "What do you call those birds in
Italian?"

"What birds?"

"There! Making all that racket!" Miss Crosby pointed
out to sea with her book, *First Lessons in Italian Conversation*. "Ever since we've been passing Sardinia."

"Didn't you ever see seagulls before?"

"I just want to know the Italian."

"*I gabbiani*," said Gabriella.

In a moment, Miss Crosby made a face, as if she were
about to grit her teeth, and said "*Grazie*." She went away
then. Gabriella crossed her legs beneath her and sat there,
guarding Aldo.

Three members of the crew presently materialized, one

raising his gun toward the birds that were flying and calling there, shifting up and down in the light.

"No!" cried Aldo in his sleep.

In two minutes he was up shooting with the sailors, and she was merely waiting on him.

"Terrible responsibility to be coming into property—who knows how soon!" said Mama.

"It's nothing to be sneezed at," said Gabriella. A white triangle of salve—Maria's Harry had tucked that into her suitcase—was laid over her nose; the rest of her face still carried a carnation glow.

Just those three sat propped on the back of the rearmost bench—Gabriella, Aldo Scampo, and Mama. They could see the long blue wake flowing back from them, smooth as a lady's train.

"Look at the dolphins!" cried Aldo.

"Where, where? Wanting their dinner. A terrible responsibility," said Mama. She ran her loving little finger over the brooches settled here and there on her bosom, like St. Sebastian over his arrows. If she had had to slap Gabriella at the lunch table for getting lost on her morning walk, all was *delicato* now. Nice naps had been taken, tea was over with, and real estate in the vicinity of Naples had come up in conversation.

"And tomorrow, Gala Night," said Mama. "Am I right, Mr. Scampo?"

"Yeah, Mrs. Serto, I guess you are," said Aldo.

Mama slipped down from between them to her feet, her fingers threw them a little wave that looked like a pinch of salt, and she began a last march around deck. Her opposite turn was the public room, where her friends would by now be collecting, the *indisposti* propped deadweight

among them but able to listen, and the well ones specu-
lating peacefully out of the wind.

When Mama passed the bench again—really her farewell time, and then she would leave the sunset to young
sweethearts—all seemed well. With the obsessiveness that
characterizes a family man, Aldo was drumming a soft
fist into Gabriella's plump young back, which held there
unflinchingly, while her words came out in snatches with
the breath cut off between.

"Nothing to be sneezed at— We'll have to wear paper
caps—and dance—"

The wake of the ship turned to purple and gold. The
dolphins, in silhouette, performed a rainbow of leaps. Gabriella screamed and her laugh ran down the scale.

Mama bowed herself into the public room, where the
mothers were expecting her, the full congregation; and
taking the seat by Mrs. Arpista, she continued with the
subject she loved the best—under its own name, now: love.

But the day of Gala Night broke forth with a trick
from the Mediterranean. Its blue had darkened and
changed, and here and there at the edge of things could
be seen a little whitecap. Father did not look too cheer-
ful at Mass, and among other sad messages coming in
from either side to Mama was the one that Aldo Scampo
himself had not been able to rise. When a wave was seen
at the glass of the porthole, looking in the dining room
at lunch, Mama retreated upward to the public room,
with Gabriella to sit by her side; and through the afternoon she declared herself unanswerable for the night.

But when the dinner gong was sounded, Mrs. Serto
found she could raise her head. She believed, if she were
helped to dress up a little . . . After she had pinned and
patted Mama together, Gabriella got out of her skirt, into

her blue, and up on her high heels; then she guided Mama down that final flight of stairs.

And when they had crossed the dining room to the Serto table, one of the old, old ladies was sitting in Mama's place. Was it simply a mistake? Was it a visit? She was far too old to be questioned. Every little pin trembling, Mama sat down in Gabriella's place, which left Gabriella the vacant one, with Mr. Ambrogio between them. The first thing the waiter brought was the paper hats.

The old lady put on hers, and so did they all after her. Gabriella's was an open yellow crown, cut in points that tended to fall outward like the petals of a daisy. But poor Mama could not take her eyes away from the old lady who sat in her place.

She was a Sicilian. With her pierced ears and mosaic eardrops, the skin of her face around eyes and mouth like water where stones have dropped in, her body wrapped around in shawls and her head in a black silk rag—and now the paper hat of Gala Night atop that, looking no more foolish there than a little cloud hanging to a mountain—their guest was so old that her chin perpetually sank nearly to the level of the table. She treated their waiter like dirt.

He was bringing every course tonight to the old lady first, instead of to Mama, and with a croak and a flick of the hand the old lady was sending it back—not only the *antipasto*, but now the soup. She wanted to see something better. Their waiter treated her dismissals with respect—with more than respect; some deeper, more everlasting relationship was implied.

And suddenly, as the *pasta* was coming in, their longmissing table mate chose to make his appearance. Another chair had to be wedged between the old lady's and Mr. Fossetta's, where he sat down, with pale cheeks, snow-white hair, and mustaches that were black as night. He looked at them all in their paper caps. His first words were to demand, "Is it true? There is no one for Genoa but me?"

Mama looked back at him, in a little soldier hat with a tassel on top, and said, "This boat is *Pomona*, going to *Napoli*."

"And after *Napoli*," said he, "Genoa." A paper cap was put in his hand by the waiter, and he put it on—it was a chef's cap—and lowered his head at Mama. "Genoa I leave only on holiday. Only for pleasure I travel. Now I return to Genoa."

"Please," said Mr. Ambrogio politely, "what is there beautiful in Genoa?"

He was handed a calling card. Mama's little hand asked for it, and she read to them in English: "C. C. Ugone. The man to see is Ugone. Genoa."

"For one thing, is in Genoa most beautiful cemetery in world," said Mr. Ugone—and did well to speak in English; otherwise who could have understood this voice from the north tonight? "You have never seen? No one? Ah, the statues—you could find nowhere in *Italia* more beautiful, more sad, more real. Envision with me now, I will take you there gladly. Ah! See here—a mama, how she hold high the little daughter to kiss picture of Papa—all lifesize. See here! You see angel flying out the tomb —lifesize! See here! You see family of ten, eleven, twelve, all kneeling lifesize at deathbed. You would marvel how splendid is Genoa with the physical. Oh, I tell you here tonight, you making a mistake to leave this boat at Naples."

Mama returned Mr. Ugone's card.

"I go to Rome," Mr. Ambrogio said.

"Say, mister," said Poldy. "What you say sounds worth coming all the way to Italy to see."

"*Signore*," said Mr. Ugone, turning toward Poldy—he had to lean across Mr. Fossetta and his *pasta*—"you will see this and more. Oh, I guarantee, you will find it sad! You want to see tear on little child's cheek? Solid tear?" Mr. Ugone made a gesture of silence at the waiter coming with the fish. "*Ecco!* Bringing the news! Is turned over, the little boat. Look how hand holds tight the hat. Mmm!"

"No sardine!" said Mama, ahead of the old lady, but there was no need of warning. The waiter had dropped his tray on the floor.

But Mr. Ugone, with his untoward respect for Poldy, went on above all confusion. "*Signore*, we have in Genoa a sculptor who is a special for angels. See this tomb! Don't you see that soul look glad to be reaching Heaven? Oh! Here a sister die young. See her dress—the fold is caught in the tomb-door—*delicato*, you accord? How she enjoin the other sister she die too, before her wedding day. Sad, mmm?"

"Say!" said Poldy.

"Gabriella, you please listen to me, hold tight that hat!" said Mama. "You shake your head and it goes round and round."

"I show you," said Mr. Ugone to all, "the tomb my blessed mother."

Back in the corner, old Papa had been fixing his eye on Mr. Ugone for some time. Now he blew his whistle.

"Go ahead," said Poldy. Mr. Ugone had stopped with his napkin over his heart. "He does that all the time—we're used to it."

"Of course," said Mr. Ugone, "other beautiful things

I show to you in Genoa. I enjoin you direct your attention to back of old wall where Paganini born."

"Say, what are you?" Gabriella asked him, holding her
crown on straight.

"Who's Paganini?" said Poldy.

But Mr. Ugone, who had never really taken his eyes
off Papa, waiting there still in that red engineer's cap
with his whistle raised, now rose to his feet. With the
words, "Also well-known skyscraper!" flung to them all,
he suddenly left them—almost as though he hadn't ever
come.

Mr. Fossetta brushed off his hands, and poured more
wine around. Under cover of Mr. Ugone's departure, the
old lady stole a roll from Mama's plate, and Mama
watched it disappearing into that old, old mouth. But
Mama remained throughout the evening just as nice to
the old lady as Gabriella was nice to Mama. Even when
the old lady described the Cathedral of Monreale from
front to back, and more than one time said, "First church
in the world for beauty, Saint Peter second," Mama only
closed her eyes and gave a brief click of the tongue.

"Mama," said Gabriella," are we coming back home on
this boat too?"

"No more *Pomona!*" said Mama. "We come home *Colomba*. By grace of Holy Mother it will not rock—beautiful white boat, *Colomba*."

"You are full of thoughts too." Mr. Ambrogio turned
to Gabriella. "I am still missing my tiepin. Do you feel
I will ever find it?"

"Who knows?" said Mama. "You never know when you
find something. That's what I tell my poor daughter every
morning she wants to sleep late the nice bed."

"Ah, it could have been lost into the sea—before we
start, who knows? Standing to wave at friends, from the

rail—'Good-by! Good-by!' " and Mr. Ambrogio half rose from his chair to wave at them now.

"But you're *wearing* a tiepin!" said Poldy, and laughed loudly at poor Mr. Ambrogio, who sat down; and it was true that he was doing so, and true too that he had been showing them from the first night out the way he had said good-by to all those friends he had in America.

"It is my second pin, not my first. Only a cameo." Mr. Ambrogio's feelings were hurt now. He was going eventually home to Sicily but certainly he wanted his first pin for his audience with the Pope. He asked not to be given any of the fish, which the waiter now brought in for the second time.

The boat lurched. A black wave could be felt looking in at the nearest porthole, out of the night.

"Ah, the Captain this boat—has he anywhere a wife?" cried Mama, and rolled her head toward the old lady, who gave no answer.

Poldy at once took out his papers. Hadn't Mr. Ugone's card at the table been enough?—even supposing it had not been Gala Night, with *gelati* somewhere on the way. Now Poldy was finding an envelope he had never brought out before, with an address written on it in purple ink —a long one.

"What town in Italy is that?" he demanded, and passed the envelope back and forth in front of Mr. Fossetta's eyes. Mr. Fossetta, with one sharp gesture of the hand and a shake of the head, went on taking fishbones out of his mouth.

"Can't read? That's the town they're taking me to to get married." Poldy beamed. "My sweetheart and her brother, or cousin, or whoever comes with her to meet the boat in Naples, they'll take me there. How about you, can you read?" he asked Mr. Ambrogio, but on the way to him the envelope had reached the old lady, who deposited it in her lap.

Poldy only shouted to the waiter, "Gee, I'll take another plate of that!", pulling him back by the coat. It was not only Gala Night that Poldy asked for second plates—it was every night. He enjoyed the food.

"If," Mr. Fossetta remarked ostensibly to Mama, with something a little ominous in his voice, "if she has a brother, then it will be her brother come to meet him."

"Only daughters have I ever been sent!" cried Mama —then gave an even sharper cry.

Through the dining-room door, arriving at the same time as the veal course, Aldo Scampo had entered like a ghost. Tentatively, not seeming to see with his eyes at all, he made his way through the dining room with all its caps, past the Serto table without a sign. Even after he had sat down safely in his own chair, who could speak to him? He was so white.

Papa, however, blew his whistle. This time he stood up to do it.

And instantly, another old man—the old man in the red knit cap who slept in the day by the ship's engines and had not exchanged for a paper cap tonight—rose up from the other side of the room and answered Papa, with mumbled words and the vague waving of an arm. He thought somebody had been insulted. Papa blew the whistle back at him, and then, carried away at meeting opposition at last, blew without stopping—"*Tweet! Tweet! Tweet! Tweet!*" The argument filled the dining room to its now gently creaking walls.

The head steward himself came to Papa's table—his first visit to the back of the room. Everybody but the other old man, and the old lady who was crushing a crust, like a bone, between her teeth, grew hushed.

"What is the meaning of this whistle?" asked the steward.

Old Papa, with his head cocked and in the voice of a liar, told the steward that once a little boy, long ago, was going away to America from Italy. Papa's left hand dived low and gave the air a pat. On such a big ship— and his right hand poked the whistle into the girth of the steward—the little boy might have been lost. But his papa said to him, "Never mind. Whenever you hear *this*" —and before the steward knew it, the old man had blown it again, *"Tweeeeeet!"*—"Papa." All this had the old sleepy-head raising both fists in the air and shaking them together as if he denied every word of that tale. The whistle was blowing and everybody else was shouting.

Aldo Scampo moved out of his chair and started silently out of the room the way he had come; only his yellow, pointed crown was crumpled like the antlers of a deer where, as he rose up, he had had to clutch his head.

"No *gelati?*" many called sorrowfully after him through their laughter.

"Why did he think he had to come, anyway?" Gabriella shrieked as he staggered past her. "Who's Aldo Scampo?"

"You imagine the sea is high tonight? Not at all!" The voice of a visiting Father, who was down from above for Gala Night in *turistica*, was heard over the room as the dining-room door fell to. Laughter stopped. This sea was no match at all for what might have been sent them, bearing the season of the year in mind. Up to now there was no word for it but calm. Had due thanks been sent up? Father, an Irishman, appeared to be looking around him for an immediate errand boy. Still, it was a fact, he said: by the essence of their nature, which was frail, all human beings were probably doomed to be seasick. The middle of the deep was never the spot God's children would show wisdom to go wandering over for long. Upstairs, Father said, with another look around, it was taking an equivalent toll.

Mr. Ambrogio leaned over his fork, which waited with a bite of veal the shape of a little ship itself, and spoke as quietly as Father to the Serto table at large. "I think on this ship there are people lower than us. This morning, alone on my way, I have seen other steps going down." And staring down over his shoulder, between himself and Mama, he suddenly sent his hand, fork and all, in a plumb line toward the floor. Consternation rose around the table, led by Mama's cry.

"Am I in wrong place?" A little old man got up from the nearest table and tottering with the roll of the ship began to turn himself around in the aisle. "Why nobody tell me?" That little man always thought he was in the wrong place, on the wrong ship, going the wrong way for Foggia; it always took many to reassure him. But tonight his cone-shaped hat came down nearly over his eyes.

Mr. Fossetta pushed back his chair.

"Looka my hand," he said. He held it up squarely, a small dark hand still burnished with the grease of America, as the little lost man drew near and bent his face over it, standing in Mama's way. Everybody who was near enough to the Serto table watched the hand; a few stood up. Mr. Fossetta rolled his wrist like a magician; then, with the knife from his plate, began to count off the fingers.

"*Firsta* class . . . *Seconda* class . . . *Us.*"

But a finger was left, dangling below the knife. That was seen. Mr. Fossetta got to his feet, drew silence again, and started over, this time counting from the middle finger and in Italian. When he finished, he flicked both hands apart on the empty air.

"Now you believe?" he said, but his own face had gone desperately white. "Nobody below us but the fishes." And poor Mr. Fossetta departed the way Aldo had gone, only it was to unfeeling choruses of "Champagne! *Gelati!*" For here came out the trays, sparkling all over, radiating to every table. Jumping up, Poldy raised his glass. "To my wedding!" he cried to the room, then swallowed the champagne without a stop.

Mama first pulled him down, then rose herself with her own arms stretched empty, like a prophetess.

"Mama! It's Gala Night," said Gabriella, joining her hands and looking into her mother's face.

Mrs. Serto, with a tragic look for all, toppled upon her daughter. Gabriella, struggling up just in time, caught her beneath the arms and then bore her, leaning, from the dining room. As they passed table after table, people who were eating *gelati* rose spoon in hand, paper hats a-bob on their heads, to make way.

It was thought an anticlimax, showing lack of appreciation of the night's feelings, that Gabriella came straight back. The *frutti* was just appearing. Crowned a little nearer to the ears, as though by one last sweep of a failing hand, she took back her real place at the table, where she ate her own *gelati* and then her mother's, and drank both glasses of champagne.

The old lady—as though she were the waiter's own mother, or the V.M., thought Gabriella—finally accepted his bowl of fruit, and Gabriella was allotted, from her fork, a little brown-skinned pear.

It was this old lady who remained last at the Serto table. When the others excused themselves, she was still dropping grapes into her mouth, like a goddess sacrificing a few extra tribes. Scarcely an eyelid flickered from above.

Upstairs in the public room, when the three-piece band began playing "Deep in the Heart of Texas" to start the dancing, an unexpected trio of newcomers turned themselves loose on the girls. Two looked like, and were, the radio operator and the man who brought the bouillon around the deck in the mornings; another, who had the mothers guessing at first, was placed as the *turistica* hairdresser, seen daily, after all, smoking in his doorway. Then Mr. Ambrogio, who had softly perfumed himself again since dinner, with the thin little widow from Rome, went arrowing bravely down the floor; she was the usually distracted mother of those divine, but sometimes bad, little children.

Gabriella stood in the door, in her blue dress mounted with ruffles from which the little pleats had still not quite shaken out—and suddenly she was asked to dance by Joe Monteoliveto. Maria-Pia was out of it too, then; there was no one who could not fall by the wayside tonight, and have a stranger appear in his place. Joe wore on his head a pink stack like a name-day cake, with a cherry on top. Gabriella gave him her hand. Out on the floor, under the stroke of the riding ship, they began circling together as easily as if they had sailed many a time across the sea, and were used to the waves and the way to dance over them.

Tonight was Gala Night, that was the reason—and partners were not real partners, the sea not the sea Mama had had in mind, and paper lanterns masked the lights that climbed and fell over their heads; and there was no colliding with the world. The band went into "Japanese Sandman," and as Gabriella went swinging in the arms of Joe Monteoliveto the whole round of the room, a gentle breath of wonder started after her, too soft to be accusation, too perishable to be hope. Dancing, poor Mrs. Serto's daughter was filled with grace.

The whole company—mothers banked around the walls, card players trapped at the tables, and the shadowy old —all looked her way. *Indisposti* or not, of course they knew what was in front of their eyes. Once more, slipping the way it liked to do through one of life's weak moments, illusion had got in, and they were glad to see it. How many days had they been on the water!

The mothers gently cocked their heads from side to side in time, the old men re-lit their tobacco and poured out a little *vino*. That great, unrewarding, indestructible daughter of Mrs. Serto, round as an onion, and tonight deserted, unadvised, unprompted, and unrestrained in her blue, went dancing around this unlikely floor as lightly as an angel.

Whenever she turned, she whirled, and her ruffles followed—and the music too had to catch up. It began to seem to the general eye that she might be turning around faster inside than out. For an unmarried girl, it was danger. Some radiant pin through the body had set her spinning like that tonight, and given her the power—not the same thing as permission, but what was like a memory of how to do it—to be happy all by herself. Their own poor daughters, trudging uphill and down as the ship tilted them, would have to bide their time until Gabriella learned her lesson.

When La Zìngara arrived, and took Joe Monteoliveto away in the middle of a waltz, Gabriella spread both arms and went on dancing by herself. Lighter than ever on her toes, as the band swung faster and louder into a new chorus of "Let Me Call You Sweetheart," and the very sides of the room began tapping and humming, she began whirling around in place in the middle of the floor.

Arms wide, toes in, four, six, ten, a dozen turns she went, and kept whirling, and at the end, as the cymbal crashed, she stopped. The ruffles ran the other way once, and fell into their pleats. The *Pomona* rose and fell, like a sigh on the breast, but Gabriella held her place—not falling: smiling, intact, a Leaning Tower. A shout of joy went up—even from those that the spectacle of an ungrasped, spinning girl was bound to have made feel worse. "Bravo!" shouted Father Madden, standing dangerously on a chair.

It was the stunt Gabriella was famous for in the St. Cecilia Sodality.

Whistles with toy balloons attached arrived on a dining-room tray, and were blown in every direction. For a moment Papa was missed. He would have enjoyed this!

"May I have the pleasure of the next?" Mr. Ambrogio asked Gabriella, moving a saffron handkerchief over his brow above dilated eyes.

Poldy, in the end, broke up the evening—he did not dance—by rushing in pretending to be Gene Autry on horseback and shooting an imaginary pistol at all the girls and all the boys and at all the lights in this room afloat in the night at sea.

It was as though they'd *forgotten* Palermo!

Everybody, at sun-up, crowded to the rail to turn one concerted gaze, full and ardent, on the first big black island rocks. They pointed fingers that trembled up at crags, into caves. They smiled on a man they had surprised in his frail little craft with the pomegranate-colored sail, far out in the early morning under the drop of some cliff. How fast now they were slipping through the silver light! Shafts of the clearing sun forked down from battlements higher than the ship was. The mist lifted and revealed something dim and green sliding near, something adored.

Smiling, they turned and admired one another. Everybody was dressed up for Palermo—not only the Sicilians, who would be reaching home. Gone were the shawls except on the oldest ladies—those were eternal. All about were the coats and hats of city streets; new stockings flashed in the light. Gone were the caps—there had been a felt hat on the grayest old grandfather since six o'clock in the morning.

Gabriella, though not specially in honor of Palermo, had got back into her blue. Only Aldo must still be untouched by where they were. Back in the canary sweatshirt, he was spread out in Miss Crosby's chair, not even looking when a passing cave was hailed as Giuliano's, and Joe Monteoliveto, with Maria-Pia pulling on his coattails, nearly fell overboard trying to see who was in it.

As they were being tugged into the harbor, it looked as though Palermo itself could wait no longer on the *Pomona.* One by one, bobbing out on the water's altered green, appeared tiny rowboats, and out of them presently came small, urgent cries. The boats worked their way nearer and nearer the ship, shirtsleeved arms shot up from them like flags, cries turned into names, and suddenly everywhere at once there was welcome. One boat was bringing thirteen, all fat, still unrecognized, one man in shirtsleeves rowing, the rest in a frenzy of waving.

"Enrico!"

"Achille!"

"Rosalia!"

"Massimiliano!"

The little old lady who had invited herself to the Serto

table on Gala Night was all ready to disembark. She was
the one with the limp. She made her way around deck like
a wounded bird on the ground, opening her mouth now
and then to scream "Fortunato!"

And suddenly she was answered from the water: "Pepi-
i-ina!"

Mama, rushing to look out by first one side, then the
other, was wildly excited. Her crisis last night had done
her good. She was dressed as though for Sunday. She
easily found *Signora* Pepina's relative for her—that was
his boat. No, it was that one!

"Fortunato!"

"Fortunato! I see him!" Mrs. Serto could be heard
above all the rest. "Fortunato and seven. Have no doubt.
It is he."

"Why couldn't he wait? We'll get there soon enough,"
said Gabriella.

"He is the rower!" Mrs. Serto swung her purse in a
wild arc; now her crucifix, having come unpinned once
but discovered thus by Mr. Ambrogio, was pinned back
all crooked.

"Francesco!"

"Pepi-i-ina!"

"Massimiliano!"

"But where is Achille?"

"He has had heart attack!" screamed Mama fearfully.

In the dock—now in plain view from shipboard—a
fight was going on among those who had been patient
enough to wait on shore; a big man in a straw hat who
had got past the rope was struggling in the hands of
the police. Here, crowded to the *Pomona*'s landward side,
the passengers could hear the warm, worldly sound of fist-
icuffs traveling across the last reach of water, the insults
rolling and falling on solid ground.

"Francesco!"

"Assunta!"

"Achille, Achille, Achille!"

"Pepi-i-ina!"

"*Ecco, ecco* Pepina!" screamed Mama. "Must we tell you which one is she?"

In the background, by the flagpole, Maria-Pia Arpista and Joe Monteoliveto were trying to say good-by. Maria-Pia was weeping into a silk handkerchief, and Joe was so swallowed up in a winter suit—the one from whose sleeves he had nearly fallen out—as to look entirely different from last night.

"*Moto perpetuo.*" The little man who had never been sure where the boat was taking them smiled at Gabriella, stirring the air with his black-nailed finger. He remembered her.

Gabriella nodded to him. She set her shoulders and posed beside her mother, frowning out from under her Buffalo hat, facing the dock.

"Fortunato, he is your brother?" Mama was asking the old woman at her other side. "Your nephew? Cousin? He was not your husband?"

"He is all I have," the old woman replied.

La Zìngara managed to be the first from *turistica* to disembark. She went swaying down the gangway, arms outstretched—secretly for balance, Gabriella felt, but outwardly to extend a tender greeting. Below, with his arms also outflung, waited, alas, a country clown, with red face and yellow shoes. La Zìngara had saved for this moment those two thin but brilliant red foxes that bit each other around her neck, both with blue eyes.

"Well, there *she* goes," said the voice of Aldo, a yawn

all through it. He had wandered to the rail where the three for the priesthood stood.

Gabriella did not even look at him. From Maria-Pia she had heard what all the boys called La Zìngara among themselves—*Il Cadavere.*

"You will see tomorrow," her mother told her with a nod. "It will be much more than this. These are only Sicilians. Why don't we go 'head to Naples?"

Gabriella screamed, "Where's the fire? What's going to happen when we do get there?"

"*L'Anno Santo, l'Anno Santo,*" said Mama. "But listen." She pulled Gabriella to her. "If you don't pay attention, you be like Zìngara some day—old maid! You see her neck? Then you cry for somebody to take you even to *Sicilia!* But who? I'll be dead then, in cemetery!" Mama gave a cross little laugh and pushed her away.

At last the Sicilians were all off the boat, and all their trunks and boxes and bundles had been flung down behind them, with the electric toasters and irons tied on like Christmas tags. The struggling and shouting and claiming ceased on shore, kissing and embracing fell off, and the final semaphores from the shirtsleeved arms were diminishing away. Once more the *Pomona* throbbed and moved in blue water.

"When did that Joe Monteoliveto sneak off the ship?" wondered Mama aloud, not yet going inside. "He never said good-by to me."

This sunset was the last. Gabriella stood at the flagpole and looked off the back of the ship; it moved smoothly now as if by magic.

Once—she couldn't remember how long ago—there had been some country they sailed near—Africa—with mountains like coals, and above, the scimitar and star of evening. The country had vanished like the two black men who got off in the night for Cape Verde. The moon and star tonight looked as though they had never been close together in their lives, to hang one from the tip of the other to go down over the edge of the world.

Was now the time to look forward to the doom of parting, and stop looking back at the doom of meeting? The thought of either made sorrow go leaping and diving, like those dolphins in the water. Gabriella would only have to say "Good-by, Aldo," and while she was saying the words, the time would be flying by; parting would be over with almost before it began, no matter what Aldo had in store for an answer. "Hello, Aldo!" had been just the other way.

"What d'you think you see out there?" came Aldo's voice. "A whale?"

Reflecting the rosy light, a half-denuded stalk of bananas at his feet—for Aldo Scampo had slipped off the boat in Palermo and back on again, without a word to anybody—he was where you could find him still, in the old place, eating away and turning over pages he could hardly see any longer.

She made her way slowly to his chair and sat down on the arm of it, and like a modest confession let out the weight of her side against his shoulder. He offered her a bite of his banana. Tiredly and quietly, in alternation, they ate it. His book dropped to the floor; the toe of her shoe found it and drew it under the chair. Her heel went down, almost without her knowing, on the idealized, dreaming, and predatory face of that Sicilian bandit.

"Almost over now," said Aldo into the evening.

Their thoughts had met. Curtained into her bed that night, and after Mama had fallen silent, Gabriella could go to sleep thinking of those three words. Just now she dropped her head and put a kiss on Aldo somewhere, the way she would upon a little baby.

Near them, there was a patter of applause. Without their noticing, the nightly circle of sitters had gathered outside tonight, on the warm apron of deck—their ranks thinned now, since Palermo, by a number of the solidest. The clapping was for old Papa, who had come forward to sing.

His verses were like little rags that fluttered on the wind from his frail and prancing person. He carried a willowy cane. He had saved his paper hat, which showed against the first stars, jutting like a rooster's crown. So he must have known all along he would sing on the last night.

He stepped back and came forward again, tapped his cane, and sang a verse; retired, and came back with a new one. His voice was old and light, a little cracked. Each time, they gave him back the chorus, sitting in close array, moved in nearer together than ever on the benches and on the floor, a row reclining against billowy knees and another leaning on billowy shoulders behind, as if for some strange, starlit group-photograph, to be found years later in a trunk. A girl went to the well for water, Papa sang, and a traveler jumped out and surprised her, and she dropped her pitcher.

Mama's benchful moved in closer to make room for Gabriella and Aldo. After they sat down, they joined in the chorus with everybody. Whatever the verse, it was the same chorus—in Buffalo, in New York, in California, in Naples, perhaps even in Genoa. As the song went on, Aldo turned his head and on Gabriella's moving lips returned her kiss.

If only that had been good-by! But here they still were. Mama in the next instant rapped Aldo's skull with her knuckle—the crack of her wedding ring went out all over the Mediterranean night. Mama was still not speaking to Aldo for his ruining Gala Night for her. He obediently caught up with the song. Everything was in darkness now —there were only the *Pomona*'s lights and the stars.

Presently Mama called out to ask Poldy the hour by his wristwatch, but Poldy did not reply. He was stretched on a bench nearby, face-down on his sleeve, asleep; his hair had turned to silver.

"Time for my Gabriella to say good night," announced Mama anyway.

"I'm not sleepy!" said Gabriella. "There's lots more songs!"

Old Papa tapped. This is for me, thought Gabriella, and stood up. Mama flew up beside her, boxed her ears, and pulled her out of Papa's way, calling to them all, "My youngest! Look once more my baby Gabriella! To-morrow she will be in Naples!"

"Good night!" they said, the women all embracing Gabriella and one another. "The last night—the last!" Mama kissed Mrs. Arpista back, and cried, "In Naples, who knows how soon something will happen?" Gabriella waved her hand at Mr. Ambrogio, who rose speechless from among the men, and then Mama led her away.

"Don't fall down the stairs!" called Aldo after her in a strangely discordant voice, almost as if it came from out over the water.

But old Papa, tapping his cane, brought in his circle closer. He could sing the night to sleep.

When the *Pomona* came in sight of land, it was sunrise. Sailors were lifting away tarpaulins, and hauling ropes and chains over the feet of a crowd, while joking indecipherably among themselves; for this once-secret, foremost deck had by now been discovered by everyone.

The body of the sea had been cut off. The *Pomona* sailed among dark, near islands, like shaggy beings asleep on one arm or kneeling now forever. Far ahead, Vesuvius, frail as a tent, almost transparent, lifted up under the morning. Gabriella watched it coming nearer and nearer to her. At last it was exactly like the picture over the dining-room mantel at home, which hung above the row of baby photographs and the yellow one of Nonna with the startled eyes under a mound of black hair.

Tightening her hand to a fist, Gabriella banged herself on the chest three times under Aldo's eyes. Holding his eyes wide open to keep himself awake gave him an expression of black indignation.

"Man Mountain Dean!" she wailed at him. "I'm a big girl now and I want my nourishment!" This had never failed to bring a laugh from the girls in Sacred Heart typewriting class.

But that breakfast was the one *Pomona* meal Gabriella could never remember afterwards; though she could see the tablecloth stained like a map with old wine. Surely she and Aldo had sat there, where neither had ever sat before, and eaten one meal together, in the hue and cry of what was about to happen.

Arrival in Naples was not so simple as being welcomed to Palermo. Only officials came out on the water to meet them, speeding direct by motor and climbing up on board. "*Attenzione!*" was broadcast every moment; everybody was being herded somewhere, only where? Mama, who could find the heart of confusion wherever it moved, constantly darted into it, striking her brow. And then, up in First Class as they stood in line to wait, the man who had charge of the S's couldn't find something he needed, his seal. Then Poldy's passport was lost—by the *Pomona*, not Poldy—and there was much running about, until all at once the spelling of his name, hailed through the room, seemed to clear things up everywhere. The feeling ran strong that landing would be soon. Mr. Ambrogio steered two of the ancient shawled ladies, like old black poodles, one on each arm, outside on deck and started a line at the rail. But Aldo Scampo still reclined in one of the overstuffed chairs, hideously yawning.

Half an hour later, with everybody watching from high on board, the docks of Naples in a bloom of yellow sun slid directly under their side. They could hear the first street sounds—*they* had awakened them!—the whipping of horses, the creaking of wooden wheels over stones, the cry of a child from somewhere deep in the golden labyrinth.

The gangway was an apparatus of steps and ropes. As it dropped like an elephant's trunk from the height of the ship, streams of Neapolitans came running toward it across a sweep of walled-in yard floored over with sun, with yellow trees stirring their leaves and buildings whose sides danced with light.

"Hey! Naples smells like a kitchen!" cried Gabriella; for all that couldn't be helped in life had stolen over her, sweet as a scent, just then.

"Not the kitchen on *this* boat!" said Aldo beside her.

"Where's Nonna?" screamed Gabriella. "Where's my Nonna?"

The first passengers, the priests, were already descending, fast as firemen down a pole. Then a shower of nuns went down.

And down rushed Mrs. Serto headlong. She flew from Mr. Ambrogio, who wished to offer her his arm, as if she'd never seen him before. She clopped down the slatted

steps like a little black pony, her spangled veil flying.
Then all were let loose!

And where was Mama now? Gabriella frowned down
over the rail, and could recognize nobody in the spinning
crowd but Mr. Fossetta. Looking flattened, taking long
steps, he seemed already making for Bari, dressed in a
Chicago overcoat, long, thick and green, with a felt hat
over his eyes and his lips pushing out a cigar. He did
not seem ever to have had a delicate stomach; he looked
bent on demonstrating that the most intimate crowd, when
the moment came, could tear itself apart, hurry to vanish.

Where was Aldo? He was still behind her, breathing on
first one side of her, then the other—breathing as he took
the coats both out of her arms, hers and Mama's. She
was left at the head of the ladder with only her purse
and the pasteboard box for the hat she had fastened on
her head.

"Now?" she asked him.

"See Naples and die!" he said loudly in her face, as
if he had been preparing the best thing to say.

She took a step down, and the gangway all but swung
free. Everything moved below, travelers and relatives running in and out of each other's arms, as if rendered by
the Devil unrecognizable; a band of ragged boys with a
ball; a family of dogs, another of blind and crippled
people; and what looked like generations of guides and
porters, in hereditary caps; and now moving in through
the big arched gate (an outer rim of carriages, horn-
blowing taxis, streetcars and cars reached around the Piazza beyond) a school of nuns with outstretched plates,
all but late for the boat. Loudest of all, a crowd of
little girls all dressed in black were jumping up and
down shaking noisy boxes and singing like a flock of
birds, *"Orfanelli, orfanelli, orfanelli—"* Then she felt

Aldo's step behind her shake the whole scene again, as if they were treading the spokes of a wheel, and now it began to turn steadily beneath them.

"Poldy!" Aldo hailed him from the air. "See Naples and die, Poldy! Where's your girl?"

Poldy was running up and down the dock pitching a ball with some little boys of Naples. He wore the feathered hat, the bright yellowish coat with the big buttons that had galvanized them all so on the first day at sea, before they knew all about him. He shouted back, "Oh, she'll find me! I sent her a whole dozen poses!"

Poldy's and Aldo's laughs met like clapped hands over Gabriella's head, and she could hardly take another step down for anger at that girl, and outrage for her, as if she were her dearest friend, her little sister. Even now, the girl probably languished in tears because the little country train she was coming on, from her unknown town, was late. Perhaps, even more foolishly, she had come early, and was languishing just beyond that gate, not knowing if she were allowed inside the wall or not—how would she know? No matter—they would meet. The *Pomona* had landed, and that was enough. Poor girl, whose name Poldy had not even bothered to tell them, her future was about to begin.

"Watch me!" Poldy, just below, was shouting to the little boys. "I'll teach you how to throw a ball!"

But he turned his shining face upward and threw the ball at Gabriella. It only struck the *Pomona*'s side and bounced back; all the same, she dodged and swayed, and Poldy covered his head with his sleeve in imitation shame, while the little urchins stamped up and down beside him, laughing in a contagious-sounding joy like the *orfanelli's*.

"Rock-a-bye baby!" she yelled down over their heads. "On the tree top! When the wind blows—"

Aldo, coming out of the family coats, put a grip around her neck for the last time. But even while he did it, instinct, too, told her she could not scream that way any longer. She was here.

"*Ecco! Ecco!*" came Mama's own voice, wildly excited. "*Mamma mia!*" There she was, halfway across the yard.

And where she pointed, almost in the center of everything, was a little, low, black figure waiting. It was the quietest and most substantial figure there, unagitated as a little settee, a black horsehair settee, in a room where people are dancing.

"But she doesn't look like her picture!" cried Gabriella. And her foot came down and touched something hard, the hard ground of Naples. Out of it came a strange, rocking response—as if the earth were shocked on its part, to be meeting their feet. Then the coats were bundled in her arms.

"O.K.," said Aldo. "Got to line up my stuff and try for a train. Good-by, Mr. Ambrogio!" he shouted. "Don't let 'em try to keep you over here!" And off he went, at an odd trot.

"We shall never meet again!" Mr. Ambrogio, standing at the foot of the gangway now with his arm raised like a gladiator, had found words. Then, raising the other arm too, he half ran through the moving game of ball, to be gathered in by some old ladies—just like the ones he'd been escorting across the ocean. But in his consideration he did not even knock down Poldy's stack of suitcases and cardboard boxes, neat as a little house in the thick of the disembarkation.

"Gabriella Serto! You want to stay on ship?" Mama had seized her and was taking her through the crowd. "Think who you keep waiting! You want to go to Genoa?"

Mama was first pushing her ahead, then pulling her back and shoving herself in front.

"*Mamma mia!*"

"Crocefissa!"

Mama threw herself forward and arms came up and embraced her.

Then Mama herself was set to one side by a small brown hand with a thin gold ring on it. And there was Nonna, her big, upturned, diamond-shaped face shimmering with wrinkles under its cap of white hair and its second little cap of black silk. So low and so full of weight in all her shawls, she not only looked to be seated there —she was. Amply, her skirts covered whatever she was resting on.

Nonna drew Gabriella down toward all her blackness, which the sun must have drenched through and through until light and color yielded to it together, and to which the very essence of that smell in the air—of cinnamon and cloves, bananas and coffee—clung. Raising Gabriella's chin, Nonna set a kiss on one of her cheeks, then the other. Nonna's own cheek, held waiting, was brown as a nut and dainty as a rose. She gave Gabriella an ancient, inviting smile.

"*Si*," she said. "*Si*."

As Nonna began to address Gabriella, the very first words were so beautiful and without reproach, that they seemed to leave her out. Nothing had prepared Gabriella for the *sound* of Nonna. She couldn't understand a word. Her gaze wavered and fell. A little way off in the crowd she saw the feet of Miss Crosby, raised on tiptoe beside a suitcase. *She* had learned only one thing the whole way over, *i gabbiani*. And there, poor Maria-Pia Arpista, rigid as though bound and gagged, was being carried off by a large and shouting family, who were proudest of all of

the baby's coming to meet her. But Nonna had not finished, already? Here was Mama rushing her off to the
Customs.

Afterwards, there was Nonna watching for them in her
same place, as they came out of the shed with their baggage behind them. The porter in a kind of madness—he
was an old man—had thrown their trunk over his back,
taken their suitcases, and then had seized the coats as
well, and even the little hatbox that had been swinging
since early morning on its string from Gabriella's finger,
like a reminder. Now she had nothing but her purse.

And there apart stood Papa. Nobody had come to meet
Papa. Even as Gabriella saw him, he was deciding not to
wait. Bearing on his cane, still in the same old olive-col-
ored sweater—why should she have expected that hole to
be sewed up by this morning?—he walked, with nothing
to carry, away into the widening sunlight as if he had
blinders on. He's only come home to die, thought Gabriella. All the way over, *he* might have been the oldest and
the poorest one. Mama pretended not to see him go. Her
curiosity about Papa had long ago been satisfied: he had
nobody: she knew it. It was the punishment for marrying
twice.

Nonna, when they reached her, said calmly, "We will
wait one little moment longer. A dizziness—it will pass."

Mama crossed herself, and laid her instant, tender hand
to Nonna's cheek. The porter just as instantly shed every
bit of the baggage to the ground.

"Are you seventy-six too, Signora?" he asked. But he
had meant it not disrespectfully, but respectfully, for he
stood inclined, with a musing finger against his cheek,
against a pillar he had made of the trunk dressed with
the coats. She raised her eyes to the empty *Pomona* standing over them still—not empty, for Mr. Ugone still rode

aboard, with Genoa yet to come. She could actually see him at that minute, standing at the rail with his cigar in his hand; but he did not see her. His gaze was bent and seemed lost on Poldy—still playing there with some of the little urchins, so that the dock took on the echoing sound of a playground just before dark. Maybe the surest people, thought Gabriella, are also the most forgetful of what comes next. All around was the smell of yellow leaves.

"Look what I see!" cried Mama, without ceasing to pat Nonna's cheek. "Mr. Scampo! Ah, I thought we had seen the last of him. On board ship—poor *mamma mia!*—he was passionately running after our Gabriella. It was necessary to keep an eye on her every minute."

"Her fatefulness is inherited from you, Crocefissa, my child," said Nonna.

"All my girls have been so afflicted, but five, like me, married by eighteen," Mama said—pat, pat, pat.

Aldo was coming toward them slowly, with his strange new walk of today, almost hidden by a large number of hopeful porters attacking him like flies from all sides. He did not wave; but how could he? He was loaded down. Gabriella did not wave herself, but suddenly missing the old, known world of the *Pomona*, she gave one brief scream. Nonna bent a considering head her way, as though to place the pitch.

"*That* she gets from her father," said Mama. "The *Siracusano!*"

"Ah," replied Nonna. "Daughter, where is my little fan? Somewhere in my skirts, thank you. With the years he has calmed himself, Achille? You no longer tremble to cross him?"

Gabriella said absently, "She should've seen him hit the ceiling when I flunked old typewriting."

"*Per favore!*" cried Mama to her. "Quiet about things you know nothing about, yet! Say good-by to Mr. Scampo."

Aldo had pulled a disreputable raincoat over his thick, new brown suit; even now he wore no hat, and his hair was down in his eyes. In addition to two suitcases he was carrying something as tall, bulky, and toppling as a man. It towered above his head.

Mama said, "If you think this fellow looks strong, *mamma mia*, I tell you now it is an illusion. He is delicate!"

"Only on Gala Night," protested Gabriella. "That's the one and only time he faded out of the picture. And so did you, Mama."

"We stop first thing at Santa Maria, to thank Holy Mother for one fate she saved you from!" Mama said. She shook her head one way, Nonna nodded hers in another.

"Hey! What you got in that thing, a dead body?" cried Gabriella to Aldo in good old English. She went bounding out to meet him.

"Watch out!" said Aldo, who seemed to have to walk in a straight line, by now, or fall. "You got nothing but just one trunk and those suitcases? You're luckier than you know."

"*You* watch out who you bump with that funeral coffin."

"*You* watch out how you talk about what I got. This is a musical instrument." With Gabriella there in his path, Aldo had to come to a full stop. The porters closed in in fresh circles of hope. "A cello," Aldo said, embracing it. Even one ear was being used to help hold it. "And after I rode it all the way in the bed over mine on the boat, the Naples Customs grabbed it right out the cover and banged the strings and took a stick and knocked all around inside it! I bet you heard it out here."

"What did you have in it?" called Mama.

"My socks!" Aldo shouted to Gabriella. "All my socks that my aunt knitted! It's going to be *cold* in Italy this winter!"

"Aldo, don't yell," said Gabriella. "That's my grand-mother."

"Oh, yeah. She looks pretty well to me," said Aldo. "She ought not to've tried to meet a boat in Naples, though."

"Mother—excuse me—Mr. Scampo, a shipboard acquaintance," said Mama.

"*Il Romeo? Il pellegrino, Signore* Scampo?" murmured Nonna serenely. She moved a glistening black silk fan back and forth in front of her now, in a way that seemed to invite any confidence.

"I'm just saying good-by to Mrs. Serto and Gabriella, ma'am," said Aldo.

Gabriella had clapped her hand over her mouth. She cried, "Aldo! Did you hear her? *Romeo!* First Mama thought you were Dick Tracy or somebody, the time you spent studying crime the whole way over—now Nonna is asking if you're not a pilgrim!"

"And what did *you* ever think I was?" Aldo stared at her rudely, clasping his burden round in that clumsy and painful way that made him look as though *he* were the one to wonder how people ever parted.

"Yes, *Signore?*" said Nonna. "Perhaps you will tell us?"

"Well, ma'am, what I came to Italy for, since somebody really *asks* me, is study cello in Rome under the G.I. Bill," said Aldo. "*Musicista, Signora.*"

"*Sfortunato!*" exclaimed Nonna, and gave a familiar-sounding click of the tongue.

"I already have a son-in-law in Buffalo the same!" cried Mama.

There Aldo stood before the three of them.

"Hey, Aldo. Want to see our trunk real quick?" asked Gabriella gently. She moved over to it, and the porter swept off the coats, unveiling it. The Serto trunk stood there—its size, shape, and weight all apparent, also the rope that went around it and the original lock that nobody trusted, and the name "Serto" painted on the lid in the confident lettering of a pharmacist. It did not matter that the hand of Customs had gone romping through it—it was restored now to the miracle of ownership.

"It's full of presents, I can tell you," said Gabriella.

Advice arrived almost like gratitude upon Aldo's face, as pride had come upon hers. "Then keep your eye on it till you get it home," he told her. "A fellow in New York told me they'll steal them even from over your head, in Naples. With a kind of tongs, very nifty. Running around over the rafters of the Customs shed, or even hanging over the gate as you go out. Everybody here knows about it, and don't even try to stop it."

"Shame," said Mama. "That's not talking nice about Naples."

And again, as Nonna spoke to him too, he was pulled around in a daze.

"My mother is telling you, Mr. Scampo, the human voice alone is divine," said Mama with her little chin up. "Not the screeching of cats. She is telling you there still may be time to set right your mistake—she sees you so young. Of course, in *Napoli*, she once sang with Caruso."

Nonna was looking up at Aldo. No two smiles were the

same in her face. Aldo had now turned dark red, and his head hung.

"Well, good-by, Aldo," said Gabriella in English, and he looked up already startled, as if to see someone he had never expected to see again.

"Be good," he replied formally, and momentarily setting the suitcases down, he shook hands with them all, even their porter, who joined the circle.

"Good-by, Mr. Scampo! Maybe we all meet at St. Peter's *Ognissanti*—who knows?" said Mama. That was what she'd said to everybody.

As Aldo staggered away, Gabriella reached out her hand and with her fingertips touched his cello—or rather its wrinkled outer covering, at once soft and imperious. It was like touching the forehead of an animal, from which horns might even start; but indeed, the old lady's withered and feminine cheek had felt just as mysterious to Gabriella's kiss. Aldo's back grew less and less familiar with every step, while the porters like a family of acrobats were leaping and crying in chorus, "*Stazione! Stazione!*" all around him. They all saw him pass, unrobbed and unaided, through the archway into the big Piazza, and away into the sliding life of the streets, and then Mama brought her handkerchief up to her face like a little nosegay of tears. *She* was being the daughter—the better daughter.

But Nonna was still the mother. Her brown face might be creased like a fig-skin, but her eyes were brighter now than tears had left Mama's, or than the lightning of bewilderment that struck so often into the eyes of Gabriella. Surely they knew everything. They had taken Gabriella for granted.

"Come now," Nonna said.

She stood up. She was smaller than Mama, she came

only to Gabriella's shoulder. But as she turned around, a motion of her hand, folding shut the little fan and pointing away with it, told them they were none of them any too soon. She stood perfectly straight, and could have walked by herself, though Mama, with a cry of remembrance, seized hold of her. Gabriella took her place a step behind. The porter once more—he, one man, all alone, and possibly for nothing—shouldered the backbreaking luggage of women, to which now something extra was added —the little rush-bottomed fireside stool on which the old lady had been sitting. They all set off toward the gate.

Only for the space of a breath did Gabriella feel she would rather lie down on that melon cart pulled by a donkey, that she could see just disappearing around the corner ahead. Then the melons and the arch of the gate, the grandmother's folding of the fan and Mama's tears, the volcano of early morning, and even the long, dangerous voyage behind her—all seemed caught up and held in something: the golden moment of touch, just given, just taken, in saying good-by. The moment—bright and effortless of making, in the end, as a bubble—seemed to go ahead of them as they walked, to tap without sound across the dust of the emptying courtyard, and alight in the grandmother's homely buggy, filling it. The yellow leaves of the plane trees came down before their feet; and just beyond the gate the black country horse that would draw the buggy shivered and tossed his mane, which fell like one long silver wave as the first of the bells in the still-hidden heart of Naples began to strike the hour.

"And the nightingale," Mama's voice just ahead was beseeching, "is the nightingale with us yet?"